O9-ABF-296

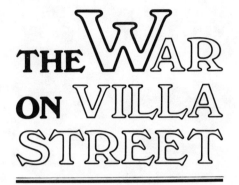

THE WAR ON VILLA STREET

Also by Harry Mazer

GUY LENNY

SNOW BOUND

THE DOLLAR MAN

THE SOLID GOLD KID
(with Norma Fox Mazer)

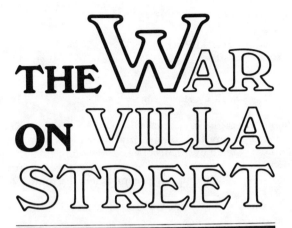

THE WAR ON VILLA STREET

A NOVEL BY

HARRY MAZER

DELACORTE PRESS/NEW YORK

Published by
Delacorte Press
1 Dag Hammarskjold Plaza
New York, N.Y. 10017

Manufactured in the United States of America
First printing

Designed by JoAnne Bonnell

Library of Congress Cataloging in Publication Data

Mazer, Harry.
The war on Villa Street.

SUMMARY: A teen-age boy tries to come to terms with
various aspects of his life: his relationship with his
often drunk and abusive father, the menace of a local
bully and his gang, and his love of running.
[1.   Fathers and sons—Fiction.   2.   Running—Fiction]
I.   Title.
PZ.7M47397War   [Fic]   78–50454
ISBN 0–440–09349–X

TO NORMA, WHO BELIEVED

THE WAR ON VILLA STREET

CHAPTER 1

Coming home from school, Willis Pierce ran his accustomed route, going down side streets and along East Broadway to make the half-mile walk a mile run. It was a warm, windy March day. The wind was against Willis, but he ran hard all the way, pushing himself. His chest filled, his heart expanded, his shirt flattened against his body. He ran so hard that the only sound he heard was the steady *slap slap* of his feet, and his heart breaking high and hard in his chest.

On Villa Street the wind whistled down the sides of the old weathered brick buildings. The Pierces lived at 55 Villa Street on the sixth floor. The apartment was empty when Willis entered. He was hungry and went straight to the kitchen. He spread peanut butter thickly on white bread, sliced dill pickles, and poured a glass of milk. Willis had a wiry frame, with skinny muscled arms and legs, and he was hungry all the time.

He stood by the window, eating and drinking, looking down into the street. Then he caught himself counting cars passing below. He turned away and flipped on the TV. Hollow, excited voices filled the emptiness in the apartment. He turned the TV on high and went into his bedroom. For some reason, today he was thinking about Mike. Maybe it was the weather. He and Mike had had plans to sleep out that spring when they were friends.

He began chinning himself on the bar across his closet. Twenty-five were easy. The next twenty-five, harder. Wonder what kind of shape Mike's in, he thought. Taller than me? Most of the guys in Willis's eighth-grade class were taller, but none of them were as fit as he was. He stood sideways in front of his bureau mirror, bending his arm to make his muscles stand out.

Mike must be 14 now, too, so that meant it was four years ago they were friends.

The Pierces had been living over on Oak Street then, above the old cemetery, and Mike was the landlady's son. The first day they moved into that apartment, he and Mike had clicked. They did everything together, went to school in the morning together, waited for each other after school. Willis would wake up in the morning and feel good just thinking he'd soon see his friend Mike.

He'd never had a friend before. Never had one since. He could still remember the day Mike wasn't waiting in the morning, or after school. The awful sick feeling in the pit of his stomach. As if he knew what was going to happen.

As soon as he got home he'd gone to Mike's apartment. Mike's mother had answered the door. She'd always had a smile for Willis. But that day there were no smiles. "Go away," she said. "Mike isn't playing with you anymore." And that evening she came to their apartment and told his mother she didn't want the Pierces in her house. She wanted them to move out.

They were always moving. They'd lived on Front Street, Oak Street, Midler Avenue, Sixth Street, Garmon Place, Coal Street, and more places before Willis could remember. He was always an outsider. And on the street, in school, even in the neighborhood grocery store, he was on guard for a snub or some dumb-ass remark about his father. He was a loner, just stuck to himself, figured things out for himself, minded his own business. Never asked anybody for anything. It was the best way.

The front door slammed. "Willis?" His mother was home. He went into the living room to greet her. "Here," she said, putting two little white bags on the table, "I brought you something." Doggie bags with leftovers from Stauffer's, where she was a waitress. Meat in one bag, sweet cakes in the other.

She emptied the cakes onto a plate, folded the doggie bags into a drawer, and put the meat in a covered plastic dish. Everything out of sight before his father came in. His father called the stuff his mother brought home "food for the dog."

"None of it has been touched," his mother said, as if she were talking to his father. "I only take the part they don't touch." Willis nodded. "Anyway, part of it is my own meal," she added. She sank down in the chair by the window. "Hand me an ashtray, Willis," she said, sighing deeply. "I'm bushed, and I've got to go back to work at six." She was heavy boned, always a little overweight, always a little tired. She lit a cigarette and said, "Listen, Willis, I want you to meet your father after work, and—"

"Mom," Willis protested. He knew what was coming.

"It's payday," she said. "We need money. Look at your sneakers. And that jacket. The holes have got holes in them. Tell him forty dollars at least."

"I don't want to go," Willis said. He'd been on these errands before and hated them.

"Get the money," his mother said. "Get the money. You know we've got to get the money before he starts drinking." In the light from the window the smoke wreathed up through her wiry black hair. "Don't you care?"

"Okay," he said, turning to the door. "Okay! Okay, I'll go."

"Willis . . ." She straightened up. "Try to get him to give you the whole envelope."

"Sure! I'll make him turn over all the money, and then I'll give him a receipt!"

Before she could say anything else he was out of the apartment and down the stairs, down five flights of stairs and out into the slap and roar of Villa Street. He'd said he'd do it, now he didn't want to think about it anymore. He ran down Villa, out to East Broadway, sidestepping a fire hydrant, veering alongside a car. He ran, he flew, and then he was floating, the air like chalk, buildings and bushes floating slowly by. He was moving effortlessly, he felt nothing, heard nothing, his feet barely touched the pavement, his legs slid smoothly back and forth.

Running was the only thing that saved him. Running every day. A mile, two miles, four miles, secretly and alone. Nobody knew how much or how fast he ran, not even Mr. Weber, who'd been after him all year to sign up for the track team. He'd never join the team. Never run where they could see him. Never give anyone the chance to point at him—*Look at him go! Willis Pierce, the drunk's son.* The faster he ran, the more they'd point and laugh. *Runs like his old man is after him.*

Willis stopped across the street from Consolidated Fabrications, a cluster of rusty green factory buildings where his father worked. It was still early. Too early for his father to come out, and too cold to hang around on the street. He circled the fenced parking lot. In back of the factory he found an open door and slipped in. He stood for a moment inside the door, letting his eyes get used to the dimness. Around him was a litter of parts and boxes, dusty pipes, and steel plates. The air shook with the pounding of massive presses and the whine of pneumatic wrenches.

"Hey, kid!" A blotchy-cheeked little man no taller than Willis beckoned to him from between two crates. Nearby stood a wheeled bin with brooms, a mop, and pails. "What're you doin' here?" the little man said. He was leaning on a broom. "They don't allow no kids in here."

"I'm looking for my father."

"Father! This place is full of fathers. I'm a father. Every guy in this place, nearly, is a father. They wouldn't be here if they wasn't. Only a father would be dumb enough to stay in this hellhole. What's his name?"

"Raymond Pierce."

"Ray-mund! I never heard him called Raymund before. Frenchie's who you mean, right?" He threw back his head as if he were swallowing a drink. Then he licked his lips. "Ummm, don't he love his bottle." He patted Willis's arm.

Willis jerked away. "Nothing personal, kid," the man yelled after him.

A burst of light caught Willis's attention. His father, wearing a pair of burnt black engineer's boots, wriggled out from beneath a long steel frame, dragging a tangle of welding cables.

"Hey, Pop."

"You!" His father stood up. He was a small trim man. "What are you doing here?" But he knew. He grimaced. "It must be that day again." He snapped the twisted welding cables straight along their length before coiling them expertly. Then he emptied his pockets. Wallet, change, and keys on top of the toolbox. The unopened brown pay envelope bulged in the wallet.

"Pop." Willis pointed to his ragged sneakers. "Mom needs money." He poked his fingers through the torn pockets of his jacket. Begging almost. He felt ashamed.

"Sit down. Get out of the aisle."

Willis sat down next to the toolbox where he could keep an eye on the pay envelope.

His father removed his greasy brimless cap and his work shirt. His chest and arms were white and bony. Bony just like me, Willis thought. A faded blue heart was tattooed on his father's right forearm with ribbons and a dove. When he was little, his father sometimes made the wings flutter for him by working the muscles in his arm.

"How's school?" his father said.

Willis shrugged. "Okay." His father had grown up in Quebec. When he'd been fourteen he'd left school and left home, gone from French Canada to English Canada. For two years he'd worked in VanHoven's Wreckers in Kingston, Ontario, then he'd gotten restless and crossed the border into New York State. He'd worked in Watertown for a year, then gone farther downstate to Schenectady, where he went to welding school. For a couple of years after that he'd drifted around central New York, taking welding jobs of six months or a year, then moving on. He'd stopped drifting after he met Willis's mother.

"Learn the language good," he was always telling Willis. "Listen to what they say. Don't grow up to be the dumb ox like me." But as far as Willis could see, except for the drinking, his father had done okay, even if he had left school in eighth grade.

"How you doing on your examination?" his father said.

"Good." *What examination?* he thought. It was only March, no exams till June. That was how much his father listened to him.

"Good, ay?" Standing barefoot on a paper towel, his father gathered his street pants tightly around his narrow waist, then put on

his shirt, fumbling with the buttons. The tips
of his first and second fingers on the left hand
were gone. "A medal," he always said when it
was noticed, "from when I work in the loco-
motive plant in Schenectady."

His father glanced out in the aisle. "Look
out," he warned, as a big fat man came rushing toward them. "Big Smitty. The foreman.
Not a word!"

"Hey, that your kid?" Big Smitty said
hoarsely. He was so fat he couldn't catch his
breath. "You know the kid don't belong in the
plant. It's against company rules. I could report you." Big Smitty looked over his shoulder,
as if he were being watched himself.

Willis's heart sank. If his father lost his job
because he'd stupidly come into the factory!
But his father looked undisturbed. He pointed
to the work he had completed that day, a dozen
iron frames squared and stacked high on the
side.

"Count them," he said to the foreman. "See
if I do a good day's work." He lit a stub of a
cigarette and added so only Willis could hear,
"Watch his lips move when he counts."

Big Smitty walked slowly around the frames,
counting audibly. He couldn't find anything
wrong, so he picked up a short length of

threaded pipe from the floor and bellowed, "Know what one of these nipples costs the company? A buck five right there, and you throw it around like nothing."

"I'm crying all over the floor," his father said.

Red in the face, the foreman tossed the pipe into the box and stalked off.

His father winked at Willis as he handed him his lunch pail. "See, they can't say nothing to me. I'm too good. I'm the best welder here." He gestured over his shoulder. "The other welders they got, they weld like chicken droppings."

Willis smiled. His father could do anything with his hands, shoot a gun, skin a rabbit, fix a motor. And anyplace he worked he was always the best.

Willis swung his father's lunch pail against his legs. The way his father had stood up to that fat foreman, he was nobody's fool! All at once Willis felt sure everything was going to be okay. His father wasn't going to start drinking. They'd take the bus home together, maybe buy a loaf of fresh Italian bread on the way. Then his father would hide his unopened pay envelope just to tease his mother. And when she came home, he'd say, *What envelope? I put it right here on the table.*

Willis breathed in deeply. Even the rough acrid smell of the factory appealed to him now. The five-o'clock horn blasted. Workers exploded into the aisles, pushing and shoving. Swept along, Willis lost sight of his father. Workers streamed past the time clocks, down a long dark tunnel, and out into the parking lot. Standing by the outside gate, Willis looked around for his father, ready to laugh with him at the way he'd been caught in the rush.

He shaded his eyes, looking back toward the factory, then across the street, just in time for a glimpse of his father's small trim head as he disappeared into Pete's Grill. "Shit!" He felt like throwing down his father's lunch pail. He crossed the street, cut around the gang near the entrance to Pete's, and pushed in. He'd been in these bars before. He hated the dank maltish smell, the phony laughter, the stupid talk.

His father was sitting at the far end of the bar, already hoisting his first whiskey. The shot glass shaking slightly in his hand, he nodded to another man, then emptied it. "Hah!" he exclaimed and reached for a beer. He swallowed a second whiskey. The torn pay envelope lay on the counter beside him.

Willis walked over and slapped the lunch

pail against his leg. The other man nudged his father. "Frenchie, that your boy?"

His father glanced around. "Go home," he said.

"Mom needs money." Willis slung the lunch pail down toward his chewed-up sneakers. He wasn't going anywhere without some money for his mother. He stared at the back of his father's head where the dark line of the welding cap still creased his skin. He was furious with himself. He'd let himself be taken in by his father's winks and jokes. Not for the first time. He was always going up and down with his father's moods.

"Pop, the money!"

His father's back twitched. He grabbed a five-dollar bill from the bar and thrust it at Willis.

Willis waited. "Not enough," he said. He wanted money, more money, plenty of money. That's all he wanted from his father. Money. No jokes, no winks, no buddy-buddy stuff.

His father fumbled more bills, smacked them into Willis's hand. "Okay, now you get out of here."

Willis walked out. Lights were coming on all along the street. People were hurrying home to the brightness and warmth of their families and supper. He knew there would be nobody home in his house. His mother would have gone back to work and wouldn't be home till late. And once his father started drinking there was no knowing when he'd come home. Willis stopped and counted the money. Twenty-five dollars. He carefully buttoned the bills into his shirt pocket. Then he ran, ran hard again, ran to shake loose the lump that had lodged itself solidly in his stomach.

CHAPTER

Hours later, a dull pounding woke Willis from sleep. *Booom . . . booom . . . booom . . .* He burrowed deeper under the blankets in his bed. *Booom . . . booom . . .* The sound was hollow, muffled, unceasing. "No," he groaned. He wanted to sleep, but it was Friday night, his father had not come home, and now he was out in the hall banging on the door. Banging to be let in. Damn him. Willis pushed aside his covers. He knew his father. He wouldn't stop his banging and kicking till Willis let him in.

He sat up, rubbing his knuckles nervously up and down the tense ridge of muscles over his stomach. Where was his mother? Why wasn't she home? Working late was no excuse! She could handle his father. She could make him do anything, except stop drinking.

The hammering stopped. Willis's eyelids drooped. He had to stiffen himself to keep from falling back to sleep. What was he doing now? Sleeping outside the door? If the neighbors found him out there they'd call the police. They'd done it before when his father, unable to make it all the way to the apartment, had collapsed on the stairs.

The banging started again. Willis scratched his head furiously. He itched all over. His mother had to come home from work earlier! He needed his sleep. He threw the blanket off his shoulders, kicked it across the floor, and went to the front door.

He could hear his father's heavy breathing through the door, hear him mumbling his mother's name monotonously with each thump. "Louise." *THUMP.* "Louise." *THUMP.* "Louise." *THUMP.*

Willis looked down at his bare feet, remembering the cold white night his father had stood at the door without shoes or socks, one crooked toe black where a piece of iron had smashed his foot. With a quick twist of the lock he threw open the door. His father, coat open, arms flailing, fell into the apartment. "Ehh, ehhh, ehhh." Like a dumb animal. Bringing with him the damp hall smell, the smoker's smell, and the pukey-sweet drinker's smell. Willis shut the door behind him. He brought his father a glass of water from the kitchen.

"Here, Pop." He held the glass at arm's length and kept a careful distance between them. His father drained the water in one long pull.

His father brushed a lock of hair from his face. Willis felt a pang of fear—his own gesture. A dozen times a day he brushed his hair from his eyes in the same way. Were they alike in every way, he and his father, he and this drunken, sloppy man?

Holding his sagging pants, his father went stiffly to the bathroom, then returned to the kitchen, where he clumsily lit a cigarette. He sat at the kitchen table, knees crossed, holding an elbow, puffing on the cigarette. He wasn't so bad tonight. Willis looked into the stove. "Mom left spaghetti and sauce." He served his father, pushed bread next to the plate of food.

"Go on, Pop, eat. It's going to make you feel

better." If he ate a little, maybe he'd go to sleep.

Willis glanced at the clock. It was nearly one o'clock. He began spoon-feeding his father. "Good, Pop? You like it?" He yawned uncontrollably.

Suddenly his father knocked his hand aside, spraying spaghetti and sauce over everything. Willis brushed furiously at the mess down the front of his underwear. His father had made a mess of himself, too. He pulled a crumpled handkerchief from his pocket, spilling a handful of bills to the floor. Willis kicked the money under the table. His eyes were burning.

"Come on! Go to bed." To his surprise his father rose and shuffled to the bedroom. It was bare and neat as his mother had left it. There was a Jesus with a red heart over the bed with dried Easter fronds behind the frame.

"Get on the bed, Pop, take off your shoes. Good boy," he said as his father sat down on the bed. "You're doing real good. Ma's going to be home in a few minutes."

His father groaned, a heartrending sound. "Pop, what is it?" His father was crying. His tears got Willis right in the gut, and he forgot to be careful. His father's hand fell heavily on Willis's shoulder. "Hey, Pop. You're hurting me." He tried to shake free. Fingers dug into flesh. His father shook Willis.

"Lies," he mumbled. "Lies, lies, lies. You told Mama I was a thief. You, Armand, my own brother."

"Pop, it's me, not Uncle Armand."

"Liar!" Often when he was drunk his father would fall into a rage over things that had happened years before. Willis's Uncle Armand was a teacher in Montreal. His father and Uncle Armand had never gotten along when they were boys. Uncle Armand had been their mother's favorite, even after they grew up and it was his father who sent money home regularly to his mother.

"Hypocrite!" his father exclaimed. He hit Willis across the face. Willis broke free, but his father came after him. Willis grabbed a chair, thrust it in front of him. He should have just run. His father pinned him against the wall.

"Lies, lies," he growled, digging the back of the chair into Willis's ribs. Willis could hardly breathe. Tears of pain and rage sprang to his eyes. "Pop, it's me, Willis! Your son, Willis, it's me," he cried.

A look of uncertainty crossed his father's face. The pressure on the chair relaxed. Rubbing his eyes, his father slumped down on the edge of the bed. "Sorry, my son, sorry," he said. "I'm so bad, so bad, so bad."

Choking, trying to catch his breath, Willis held his ribs and limped out of the room.

CHAPTER 3

The house was filled with a gray silence. Willis lay in bed, unmoving, listening to the squeak of the bed in his parents' room, then the creaking of the floorboards as his father crossed barefoot to shut the window. It was Saturday, so his father must be working overtime. Good thing. They could use the money. For the occasional Saturday's extra pay, his father would get up, no matter how rotten he felt. He could be sick to his stomach, eyes puffed shut, unable to swallow a mouthful of food—still, he'd go to work.

His mother was up now. A bureau drawer slid shut. Water ran in the bathroom, loud in the toilet, soft in the sink. His parents rarely talked in the morning. His father hacked, his mother sneezed. Cat sounds—*chee, chee, chee* . . . ten *chees* before she stopped.

Willis got out of bed. His ribs ached. His shoulder was black and blue. He did his push-ups, but slowly. After he was dressed, he sat on the bed, hungry, but not leaving the room till he heard the front door click behind his father.

His mother was in the kitchen smoking, an ashtray on her lap. Her eyes were puffy, barely open. "You have a bad time last night?" she said.

Willis touched his ribs. "I fed him the spaghetti."

"I saw the garbage." She sighed.

Willis sat down. They never talked much, but they understood each other. Willis knew how his mother felt about him. She loved him, but she didn't have to worry about him. She had to worry about his father. He gave her the twenty-five dollars he'd collected from his father, then looked under the table. "Did you get the other money?"

"Twenty-three dollars," she said. "There's a dollar for you under the plate."

She made him a couple of scrambled eggs. When he shook on the ketchup he felt the ache in his shoulder. Remembering, his face filled, his eyes moistened. He turned away from his mother so she wouldn't see.

When he finished eating he stuffed the dollar in his pocket and went out. His eyes were burning from not enough sleep, and his arms and legs felt heavy and separate from his body. He walked over to Sunset Parkway, forcing himself to keep to a brisk pace, then broke into a run near Eamon's gas station. It was already choked with cars and people. He ran steadily down the Parkway, alongside the creek. Gradually, the lethargy lifted, and by the time he'd run two or three miles his eyes had stopped burning.

Around noon he bought himself a slice of hot pizza at the Pizza Shed and ate it standing at the counter. He was so thirsty after that he went into a grocery store and bought a quart of milk and drank it down without stopping. He had nowhere special to go, and stopped by the Prescott Street playground to see if anyone was looking for a game.

Prescott playground was one of the really old playgrounds in the city. One side was for

23

little kids, with sandboxes, swings, and slides, and the other side was marked off for basketball and handball. Some kids were tossing a ball around, but Willis didn't know them. He hung around for a while, wondering if they'd need another man. He loved ball games, baseball, basketball, stickball, softball, it didn't matter. What mattered was playing as hard as he could, and then, after, the good thick hot feeling he had when he was sweaty and his hands were swollen and hard.

After a while he sauntered away, hands jammed into his pockets. Maybe he'd go to a movie, maybe just go home and watch some TV. In the alley between the playground and Nedman's fruit store, he nearly stumbled over Rabbit Slavin and his gang, Bucky Spivak, Kinsella, and Sam Viglione. They were bunched together, boosting a big kid up on a garbage can, yelling at him to reach higher. Willis guessed they'd been playing handball and someone had hit the ball up onto Nedman's high flat roof. He leaned against a building, idly watching the action.

"Get the monster up there," Rabbit Slavin ordered. His henchmen gave the big kid a shove.

"Oh, no, I'm going to fall," the kid moaned.

Willis recognized him as Richard Hayfoot, one of the retards from the Special Ed class. He was a tall, soft-looking boy with gold-rimmed glasses. "Rabbit, can I get down?" He was wearing a blue jacket and white sneakers, and a white cap. If you just looked at his clothes you'd never know anything was wrong with him, but one look at his face and that was it. He had a big loose mouth that was always half open, and usually this dumb smile on his face. The reason Willis knew him was because he hung around the playground for hours, begging for games.

"Rabbit! Rabbit, is it okay if I get down, please?" he cried.

"Shut up. Monsters don't speak." Rabbit punched his legs a couple of times.

The retard clutched the wall, looking scared to death. He was older than Willis, older than any of Rabbit's gang, who were all a grade ahead of Willis. Richard was 15, maybe even 16. But he might as well have been six months, Willis thought. He wasn't a real person. Just half a person, or maybe one quarter of a person. Retards like Richard bugged Willis. Some of them knew their place and stayed in it. They didn't try to mix with the normal kids. But Richard didn't even have that much sense.

Willis had seen a girl like Marion Bouchard, a really sharp girl, sitting down with Richard in the cafeteria and combing his hair like he was some kind of big doll. Willis had never even been able to say two words to Marion, but Richard had sat there blabbing away. Bla bla bla bla bla!

"Let me down, please," he bleated now. "I can't reach that high. Rabbit, Rabbit, please."

Willis regarded him contemptuously. Why didn't the big goof just get down from the garbage pail? But he knew why. Even normal kids were scared of Rabbit Slavin. There were Rabbit stories all over school. They said once he'd broken a kid's arm. Another time he'd burned a kid's butt with a cigarette. Willis didn't know for sure if those stories were true or not. But if Rabbit was your enemy, watch out.

Rabbit and his friends practically ran the whole ninth grade in Columbus Junior High. And no use expecting the teachers to change anything. Most of them liked Rabbit. He was super polite to adults, he knew how to "yes, sir" and "no, ma'am" them, smiling and showing his big bright front teeth.

"Up on your toes," he ordered the retard. "Reach! You're tall enough."

"Goose him," Bucky Spivak suggested. "Make

him fly," he brayed loudly. Willis couldn't stand that fat slob, with the grease smears on his mouth and stains down the front of his shirt. He was supposed to be a funny man, he always had something to say, but as far as Willis could make out he was just a big dirty mouth.

Richard kept bawling to come down and Rabbit finally pulled him off the garbage can. "You're useless." Then, looking around, he spotted Willis. "What are you looking so smart about, Pierce? Grab him!" he ordered.

"Hey," Willis protested, but Kinsella and Bucky already had him and yanked him into the alley. Rabbit and his big goons surrounded him.

"You got a ball on you?" Rabbit demanded.

"No," Willis said.

"Frisk him," Rabbit ordered. Sam and Bucky held him, and Kinsella turned out his pockets. No use fighting. It was four to one.

"No ball," Kinsella reported. Willis couldn't understand a guy like him being one of Rabbit's stooges. Kinsella was a real sports hero, the fastest man on the track team. He was all legs.

"Pierce is as useless as the retard," Sam Viglione said. "Right, Rabbit?" He shot Rabbit an eager look. Sam was the one who really got under Willis's skin. He was one of those handsome boys who look like they ought to be standing in the window of a clothing store with the other dummies. He had black hair and big dark lustrous eyes. Girls went crazy over him, but that wasn't why Willis despised him. What disgusted him about Sam Viglione was how he was always licking Rabbit. Lick, lick, lick.

"Put the short one on the long one," Bucky said. "Pierce on the retard, then they'll reach. No, wait, I got a better idea. Let's just throw Pierce up on the roof. He's a skinny little turd." He grabbed Willis around the back. "Come on, you guys, grab his legs!"

Willis struggled. These guys were crazy enough to try. "Let me go! I can get your stupid ball!"

"Yeah? How, big shot?" Kinsella said.

Willis's eyes fell on the drainpipe which went all the way up to the roof. He shook free and grabbed the drainpipe.

"Up the pipe?" Bucky said. "You fool!"

"Shut up, Bucky," Rabbit ordered. And then, looking meanly at Willis, "Go on. We're all waiting." Rabbit's big hands hung half curled at his sides.

Willis took a deep breath and sprang up on the drainpipe, grabbing with both hands. The pipe swayed. Willis hung there for a moment, wondering what he'd got himself into.

"Hey, Pierce, you waiting for the TV cameras?" Bucky said.

Willis went up the pipe fast, hand over hand, not even gripping with his feet. He was the only boy in Mr. Weber's gym class who could climb the ropes that way. When he reached the roof he hooked an arm over the cornice and hung there. His ribs were aching again. They were all looking up at him. The retard, fat Bucky, Sam, Kinsella with his yellow track-team jersey, and even Rabbit. They were all looking up in surprise.

Willis threw a leg over the cornice and pulled himself onto the roof. It looked like nobody had ever been here before. There were balls all over the place, plus a lot of other junk. Willis gathered all the balls together and rolled them to the edge of the roof. He shot the balls down one after the other. The boys scrambled to catch them.

Satisfied with the way he'd showed up Rabbit, Willis slid down the drainpipe. "Hey, Willis, that was good climbing, good climbing!" Richard hung over Willis, breathing damply in his face. He tried to grab Willis's hand. "Hey, Willis, you're my friend, I like you."

Willis shook the big dope off. He was too close. He couldn't stand the dumb look on the kid's face. "Scram. I'm a mad dog." He bared his teeth. "If I bite you, you'll get rabies." He would have left then, but Rabbit stopped him, a calculating smile on his face.

"That was spunky stuff, Pierce." He put an arm around Willis's shoulder. "Nobody else could have gone up that pipe." Willis stiffened, waiting. His eyes darted around watchfully. He didn't trust Rabbit as far as he could throw him. "You're a regular human fly," Rabbit said. "I liked that."

"Yeah, a regular human fly," Sam echoed.

"Tell Willis about the Avengers," Rabbit ordered Bucky. "I think he could fit in."

"Him in the Avengers?" Bucky protested. "You want me to tell Pierce about the Avengers?"

"That's what I said, isn't it?"

"But, Rab—"

"Shut up! Whose club is it?"

"Yours, Rab."

"Tell Willis about it."

"Nobody fools with the Avengers," Bucky said reluctantly, "and we don't ask just anybody to join. So I don't know why he's asking you!"

Rabbit punched Bucky hard in the arm. "Hey, what did I tell you?"

Bucky held his arm. "Jeez, Rab! That hurt."

"Go on."

"To belong, you got to be special," Bucky said sullenly. "Like, Rabbit is the manager of the baseball team."

"And even if I wasn't," Rabbit said, "it would still be my club because I'm Rabbit Slavin."

"That's right, that's right." Sam danced eagerly around Rabbit. "You made it up, you say who belongs."

"Shut up, Sam! Go on, Bucky."

"And Kinsella is the fastest runner in the school. I'm the class comedian. And Sam—"

"I'm the class lover," Sam said, taking out his comb and combing his dark hair carefully over his forehead.

Willis was completely taken aback. He had never even dreamed of being one of Rabbit's boys. And, despite his scorn for clubs and cliques, for a moment he allowed himself to imagine being one of the gang. He couldn't stand Bucky and Sam, but maybe he and Rabbit and Kinsella would become a threesome.

"We take turns at each other's houses," Sam said eagerly. "Don't we, Rab? Whosever house it is supplies the eats."

"If we let you join, it'll be your house next week," Rabbit said.

Willis's scalp tightened. That did it. No one

came to his house. No one. Never. No way. Because he never knew when his father might be home and so out of it he couldn't even say hello. Or staggering around mumbling to himself about his brother Armand. Or smelling of puke.

"No one meets in my house," he said.

Rabbit's head snapped up. His big buggy eyes pinned Willis down. "What'd you say, Pierce?"

Willis stepped back. He wished he could get away. Nobody turned down Rabbit, or anything Rabbit wanted, the way he just had. He tried to think of something to say to cover up, an excuse or a reason Rabbit would accept.

"Maybe your house is too good for us, Pierce?" Rabbit said.

Willis shoved his hands into his pockets, then took them out. He wished he'd never stopped to watch Rabbit pushing the retard around. Rabbit's face was tight and mean.

"Hey." Kinsella pushed Willis. "Rabbit asked you something, slob." He pushed him again. "Answer!"

"Maybe he's too busy to talk to us," Bucky said. "Busy, busy man. Too busy to join our club."

"Busy," Sam said, playing Bucky's straight man. "What does he do?"

32

"You know," Bucky said, "busy busy." He made an obscene gesture with his hand. "Do that too much, and your brains rot, Pierce."

They all laughed. Richard laughed, too. Only Rabbit stood a little to one side, watching Willis, his big head tilted back, his lips half parted, as if he were sniffing something bad. All the alarms inside Willis went off. Nobody he knew or had ever heard of said no to Rabbit and lived for long.

"Hey, look! Look," Sam half whispered. Two girls had just turned the corner. Sam's black lustrous eyes shone. "Oh, man," he groaned, holding himself in mock agony. "Oh, oh, oh!"

Willis froze. It was Marion Bouchard and Susan Tyson. Marion was in white jeans and a white beaded jacket. Many times Willis had watched Marion secretly from the corners of his eyes. She was taller than he was, wore a lot of eye makeup, and had a cloud of soft dark hair. When she raised her arms in class, smoothing her hair, he could hardly tear his eyes away from her breasts. But if she caught him looking, he sneered and quickly glanced aside. He only dared watch her secretly and dream of impossible things.

"Think she's wearing a bra?" Sam whispered, smoothing his black hair.

Rabbit's teeth shone. "Wouldn't I like to get my teeth into them!"

The girls came straight toward them. Willis's cheeks flamed. The cool level look Marion gave him made him feel like disappearing. Susan Tyson, who lived next door to Sam on Front Street, pointed at him. "What'd I do now?" Sam said.

"Sam Viglione, your mother told me if I saw you, tell you to come straight home." She ran both hands through her short curly hair. "You get the message okay, or you want me to repeat it—slowly?" She and Marion left, exchanging smiles.

Kinsella and Bucky grabbed one another, groaning and telling Sam he better run right home and see what Susan Tyson *really* wanted.

"I'll run, I'll run," Richard said, causing an explosion of laughter. "Me and Willis'll run!"

The Rabbit remembered Willis and turned and gave him a long cold stare. Willis's face burned. He hated stupid Richard and his big mouth. He hated Rabbit. He hated all of them. They were all so full of shit! They thought they were *it* and could say and do anything because Rabbit's father was a policeman. But Sam's father just worked in a rug store, and Bucky's father worked in a factory like Willis's father. So what made them think they were better than him? But Willis knew, knew it in his bones. It was his father's drinking, the drinking and the funny way he talked that made him, Willis, an outsider. He turned abruptly and walked away.

CHAPTER 4

Monday afternoon Willis had just gotten home from school when the doorbell rang. His mother had left a note saying the super was coming up to fix the leaky bathroom radiator. And about time, Willis thought. He set his soda can down and opened the door. Rabbit Slavin stood there, one hand on top of the doorframe, a black walkie-talkie hanging from his belt. Without even thinking, Willis started to shut the door on Rabbit, but the bigger boy shouldered his way in.

"Who's home?" he said, looking around.

"My father's coming right up," Willis said quickly.

Rabbit laughed. He strolled into the living room, picked up a sofa cushion, and sniffed it like it was something dirty. "No wonder you didn't want the Avengers to come here," he said, tossing the pillow down. "This junk looks like the stuff you get in the Salvation Army."

Willis's stomach knotted. Now he understood what Rabbit was doing here. He'd come to get back at Willis for refusing to join his club. Willis looked at Rabbit's big hands. Would he try to beat him up in his own house? He didn't know how he would do against Rabbit. He was in shape, but Rabbit had twice the weight, twice the heft.

"How about a beer?" Rabbit said. "How about some hospitality, man?" He was Mr. Cool himself.

"There's no beer in this house," Willis said.

"Don't give me that. What're you drinking?"

"Soda." Willis shook the can in Rabbit's face. "Can you read? Hires orange soda! Look, I'm busy." He opened the front door. "Good-bye."

"Man, you're friendly," Rabbit said, shaking his head. "I don't understand you, Pierce. This the way you treat all your guests? Hey, is that the john?" He pointed to the bathroom at the end of the hall. Then, not waiting for Willis's answer, he walked in and locked the door.

Willis slammed the front door furiously. This was really incredible. Rabbit Slavin was locked in *his* bathroom! What was he doing in there, anyway? Checking their medicine cabinet? Snooping in the clothes hamper? He wouldn't put it past Rabbit to piss on the toilet seat out of pure meanness. He rapped on the door. "Come on! Get out of there!"

Rabbit didn't answer. Maybe he was calling his buddies on the walkie-talkie. That was it! He was calling Bucky, telling him everything. Making a fool of Willis. Now he was sure he heard Rabbit speaking softly. *This is Rabbit— over. . . . Observation point, Pierce's bathroom —over. . . . Chipped tiles . . . hairs in the sink . . . dirty toilet bowl—over. . . .*

The toilet flushed. Then the door was unlocked. Willis rushed in past Rabbit to see what he'd done. He put down the toilet seat with a quick glance around. "You better scram. My father catches you here, he'll break your neck."

"Is he as big and tough as you?" Rabbit said contemptuously. He sauntered down the hall and looked into Willis's parents' room. "He and your mother sleep in that double bed? Nice big bed." His front teeth glistened.

So angry he couldn't speak, Willis closed the door to his parents' room, then rushed after Rabbit, who had strolled into the kitchen. Rabbit opened a drawer.

"What're you doing? Close that drawer!"

"Doggy bags," Rabbit said. "Arf, arf! I know what you eat." He pointed to the refrigerator. "Beer in there?"

"I told you, there's no beer in this house!"

"Go on," Rabbit said, "your father drinks, your mother, too. They're both boozers."

"That's a lie," Willis choked. "Where'd you hear that lie? My mother hates the stuff."

"She works in a bar, doesn't she? Those people are the biggest boozers of all. They need it so bad they even got to work around it."

"Get out," Willis shouted. "Out! Out!"

"Hey, watch it," Rabbit said. "You get mad too easy. That can get you in a lot of trouble. You're in a lot of trouble right now, boy." He whipped the antenna out of the walkie-talkie. "Who do you think you are, anyway, telling me you don't want to join my club? Think I forgot that? That what you think? I didn't forget it!" Rabbit was really working himself up into a rage. He jabbed Willis with the end of the antenna. "You little drunken queer, don't you tell me to get out of your house. I'll get out when I'm good and ready, queer!"

He whipped the antenna back and forth in front of Willis's face, snapping it through the air. Willis suddenly darted forward and snatched the walkie-talkie from Rabbit's hand. "Hey! Give that back," Rabbit yelled.

Willis ran to the door. He was in a sweat, but aware that for the first time he had the upper hand. "I'm counting to three," he said, opening the door. "Get out of my house, or I chuck this thing down the stairs."

"That's not funny," Rabbit said menacingly.

"I'm not joking. One."

Rabbit, arms loose, moved toward him. Willis backed into the hall, keeping his eye on Rabbit. "Hand over that walkie-talkie, Pierce. You little fart, you know who you're fooling with?"

"Two," Willis said. His voice was shaking, but he kept the walkie-talkie at arm's length.

"Thr—"

Rabbit lunged for Willis. "Look out," Willis cried. The walkie-talkie fell on the floor. The black plastic cover split open.

"Look what you did," Rabbit screamed.

"You can glue it, you can glue it," Willis said. Parts were scattered down the hall.

"Glue it. Glue it! You freak, it was brand new. You're going to buy me a new one, or I kill you." Rabbit's face was swollen with rage. He caught Willis by the shirt. "You're going to pay," he shouted, banging Willis's head against the wall.

Once! Twice! Three times! Incredibly, Willis kept count as the big ape knocked out his brains. He was actually beginning to see stars when he broke free and ran into his apartment. He slammed the door, then bolted it.

Rabbit hammered at the door. "I'm going to get you, Pierce. I'll bash your head. You hear me? I'll kill you. You better watch out for your ass. From now on, you're number one on the Avengers' hit list."

Willis took his can of soda and sat down in front of the TV. He turned on the TV full volume. His head ached, but he kept the TV on till Rabbit stopped kicking the door and went away. He was shaking and cold. After a while he went into the bathroom, stripped, and stood under the shower with the water turned on as hot as he could stand it.

He stood under the shower for a long time, letting the hot water run over his head and his face and across his shoulders. It still hurt where his father had dug into his shoulder. One big thumbprint tattooed in front, and two fingerprints in back, like two purple grapes. His ribs were still sore and black and blue, too. And now, besides, he had a bump the size of an egg on his head, courtesy of Rabbit Slavin.

Rabbit's threats to get him scared the shit out of him. In the privacy of the shower he could admit it to himself. But he hadn't meant to bust Rabbit's precious toy. All he'd wanted to do was get him out of his house. It was Rabbit's fault, not his. But what difference did that make? Rabbit would be out for him now, and not just Rabbit, but all his stinking henchmen.

Willis joined his hands and tensed the muscles in his arms. He didn't like being scared. But that Rabbit was an animal. Well, if it came to that, he wasn't worried about Bucky, or Sam, or any of those freaks individually. If he ever caught that bigmouth Bucky alone, there'd be nothing left of him but a pile of grease. And if Marion Bouchard came along and watched, that would be twice as good.

After he'd taken care of Bucky he'd brag a little, show Marion the marks his father had put on him. She'd gasp. *Willis, how awful!* But he'd just shrug. *My father's one of those hot Latins.* He'd give her a special look. *Like me*, he'd say. Ha. If he had the nerve. He didn't have the nerve to even say Hi to her yet, but one of these days . . .

He was always dreaming about Marion. About Marion and him alone. Walking down the street with his arm around her. Or together in a car. Or maybe he'd go up to her house and ring the doorbell. She'd answer the door and be so delighted to see him she'd invite him in. No one would be home. Maybe that's when he'd show her his bruises. Just take off his shirt and show her. He wouldn't cry about it. Just let her see the marks. That would be enough. Girls were impressed if you were hurt. It did something to them, aroused the nurse in them. They wanted to bandage you up and take care of you.

The thought of himself stripped to the waist, and Marion's cool cool fingers, made him squirm. Maybe she'd take off her shirt, too. He'd never seen a girl naked except in pictures. Once he'd walked into an X-rated movie. No one had said anything to him. He'd sat alone in the dark, slumped down in his seat, his heart pounding like he'd just run five miles. The movie made him want to burst. He kept crossing his legs and crossing his legs, and then he couldn't hold it any longer. When he left he felt that everyone knew, the ticket collector, the usher, the people standing in the lobby, they all knew. He had walked around till his pants dried, and then he had gone home.

"Willis." His father was rapping on the door. Willis grabbed a towel and wrapped it around his waist. His cheeks were burning. His whole body was burning.

His father walked in. "You finished with that shower?" Willis stepped out of the shower. His father bent over, taking off his shoes and socks. "You leave me any hot water?" He looked up, then frowned. "What happened to you?"

Willis felt the egg on the back of his head. But that wasn't what his father meant. He gestured at Willis's body.

"Your shoulder, everywhere, you're black and blue. Are you fighting? Who did it to you?"

Willis pulled on a clean T-shirt. "You know," he said.

"Eh?" His father looked puzzled. Didn't he know? Didn't he really know? How could he forget? He'd practically killed Willis the other night.

"You did it," he said, tucking his shirt into his pants.

"Me! No, when did I do it? I never touch you."

"You never touch me," Willis repeated bitterly. "Man, when you're drunk, you lose your mind."

"Hey, what are you talking about?"

"Friday night," Willis said angrily. "Friday night! You remember now?"

His father shook his head, but he couldn't meet Willis's glance. "I did it to you?" Willis nodded. "I'm sorry," his father said. He said it again. He was sorry. Sorry, sorry, sorry. Willis didn't speak. What was he supposed to say? First they beat you up, then they apologized. Maybe Rabbit would tell him he was sorry next.

"It's the whiskey," his father said. "It makes me crazy. No more." His father raised his hand. "No more. You hear me?" He looked up, like he was promising God. "Not a drop of liquor ever again. Not even a taste, so help me Jesus."

Willis finished dressing quickly. His father was sorry, Willis could see he really meant it now, but he'd forget. Willis knew him. If only he could believe his father's promise. If only it wasn't talk. But Willis had heard these promises before. It might take a day or two, even a week or two, but his father would forget, the way he always forgot. The same way he forgot about everything.

CHAPTER 5

The late bell rang as Willis approached Columbus Junior High. The old massive red-brick building with its yards and fenced playgrounds filled a city block. Across Columbus Avenue were the track and playing field surrounded by bleachers. Willis had deliberately come to school late that morning. Thinking over what had happened with Rabbit and the walkie-talkie, he had decided that the smart thing to do was stay out of Rabbit's way till he cooled off.

Usually in the morning Rabbit held court

outside school. He'd be in the middle of a gang of boys, with his own special boys in the inner circle like a private secret service, screening the onlookers. Some of those guys were still lingering at the door. Willis stopped and bent down to tie and retie the laces on his blue-and-white running shoes. When he straightened up, everyone had gone in. Satisfied, he went quickly across the street and up the steps. The halls were nearly empty.

Hurrying past the principal's office, Willis noticed the bright-red poster tacked up on the bulletin board near the trophy case. "COLUMBUS JUNIOR HIGH FIFTEENTH ANNUAL FIELD DAY." He walked by, then swung back to read the whole poster.

COLUMBUS JUNIOR HIGH FIFTEENTH ANNUAL FIELD DAY. MAY 15.

Open to all students of Columbus Jr. High. Track and Field Events. First, Second and Third Place Ribbons to be awarded. Parents, friends, and neighbors invited to watch. This is one of our school's big events. Sign up NOW with Coach Weber. This is for EVERYONE. This means YOU.

47

"Not me," Willis muttered, studying the picture on the bottom, a guy leaping a hurdle. He wouldn't be caught dead in something like this. Every show-off in school would be there, all the hotshot athletes like Kinsella, and all the hotshot braggarts who figured they could be hotshot athletes, given half a chance.

All week the big push for Field Day was on. Announcements were made over the PA system every day by Coach Weber, then by Mr. Firstman, the vice-principal, then by kids from the eighth and ninth grades who had participated in last year's Field Day. This was the week of March 15, and there were exactly two months till Field Day, as Willis and the other students were informed at least ten times a day. Coach Weber wanted more participation. Boys and girls, seventh-, eighth-, and ninth-grade students, special students and regular students.

"Everybody but the teachers," the coach joked, his voice booming over the PA and into every room in the school. "Teachers are the only ones we discriminate against."

"Ha, ha." Willis rolled his eyes up in his head.

"You going to enter?" Buddy Ley asked him. Buddy sat across from Willis in Miss Blesch's English class. He had a voice like a frog, but he was okay, a regular kid who never bothered anyone.

"What for?" Willis said, shrugging, but he caught himself figuring which events he could take. Maybe the 220. For sure the half mile. That would make them sit up. Everyone in school would expect Kinsella and maybe Jim Williams to take the running events. And then here would come Willis Pierce, out of nowhere. The idea was so sweet he kept playing around with it, seeing himself coming in a pace ahead of Kinsella in every race. Wouldn't that get to Rabbit!

But he stopped daydreaming fast when he saw Bucky and Sam hanging around his locker. To be on the safe side he didn't go to his locker after last bell, but beat it out of school and took a different route for his run home. He stayed on the alert all the way, scanning the street ahead of him and avoiding alleyways and blind corners. Rabbit wasn't going to catch him asleep.

All week he followed the same pattern, coming to school as late as possible in the morning and leaving fast at the end of the day. He avoided the cafeteria, where he knew Rabbit hung out at noon, and he was extra careful in the halls between classes.

When he left for school Friday morning he

felt good. He'd managed to stay out of Rabbit's way so far, and just had to get through this day. The weekend was no problem, and by Monday Rabbit would be thinking about somebody else he wanted to push around. That's what Willis wanted—to have Rabbit Slavin forget he even existed.

At noon he took his sandwich and ate it outside, sitting alone on the steps. It was a cool day. He zipped up the new plaid jacket his mother had bought him, liking the way the cloth tightened around his shoulders. He was humming under his breath when a sullen-looking kid he didn't recognize came around the side of the building. "You Willis Pierce?" Willis nodded. "Rabbit's looking for you."

Willis got hot under his shirt. He stood up, crumpling his lunch bag. "Who told you to say that? Who told you I was out here?"

"Rabbit's looking for you," the kid repeated. When Willis stepped forward, he darted off. Willis looked around, the muscles in his arms tensing. He half expected Rabbit and his gang to come charging around the building. His mouth was dry.

He became aware that he was hunched over, as if he were just waiting to be hit. He straightened up. Okay, so Rabbit was looking for him. Well, let Rabbit find him then. What was he supposed to do, hide for the rest of his life? Recklessly, he wished Rabbit would show up then and there. They'd settle things once and for all.

The defiant mood stayed with him. After school he didn't hurry out, and he ran boldly down his usual streets. All the way down Columbus Avenue, across South, along the creek, and up Fitch Road. That was where the trouble happened. Fitch Road was cut through a steep hill. There was a cliff on one side, and just a few scattered houses on the other side. He was moving along, not even thinking of Rabbit, when a stone hit his shoulder. Then another stone hit him in the back. The Rabbit gang was behind him. Even then, it might not have been so bad if he hadn't turned to look at them. That was his mistake. He lost his momentum and Kinsella sprinted up and grabbed him.

Willis struggled silently with the taller boy. Then the rest of them were there, surrounding him. The redheaded Dodge twins had joined Rabbit's other stooges. "I told you I'd get you, Pierce." Rabbit gave him a poisonous look.

Willis was furious with himself. He'd been an idiot to let down his guard. And now his knees were knocking together, he was so scared. Where did he ever get the idea he could whip Rabbit? If Rabbit was a rabbit, he was a monster rabbit, with arms like baseball bats and a face as hard as a stone wall.

"Search him," Rabbit ordered. "I want his money."

"I don't have any money," Willis said, but they didn't believe him. They turned out his pockets, scattering pencils, paper, and a handful of change.

"Fifty cents," Phil Dodge snorted, picking up the money and handing it to Rabbit. "And a dirty old snot rag."

Rabbit threw the change away. "I said *money*. Where are the dollars you owe me, queer! You drink it all up?"

Willis tightened his lips, determined to say nothing. Rabbit hated him. It was there in Rabbit's mean buggy eyes, in the twist to his mouth. Willis's own mouth was dry. A guy like Rabbit, once he found your weakness, he liked to reach in and scrape the place raw, scrape it till you howled. Then he'd scrape it some more, just to hear you howl again. That was how he got his kicks. And the more you cried, the better he liked it.

"You either pay up," Rabbit said, emphasizing each word, "or I'm going to pound it out of you." He pounded a fist into his palm. "That'll be just as good."

There was no money, and no way in the world Willis could get it. And even if he had it, from the look on Rabbit's face he would take the money and pound Willis anyway. And now they started getting ready to pound him by yanking off his jacket. Willis's heart sank. His mother had paid a lot of money for that jacket. Larry Dodge blew his nose hard on it. His brother Phil bent over laughing. They yanked the jacket between them, then tossed it to Sam.

"Hey, Rab, watch this!" Sam flipped the jacket high into the air, where it caught on a limb of a tree growing on the hill.

Someone shoved Willis from behind. "Look at him stagger. He's been drinking." They shoved him back and forth, from one to the other. "Stupid drunk! Stupid drunk like his stupid drunk father." Shove! "Think you're better than anyone else, don't you?" Shove! He kept his hands up, tried to hold them off. *Don't cry,* he ordered himself. *Don't let them know you're scared.*

"All right, all right," Rabbit said, "quit fooling around. Lay it on him so he knows I'm not kidding."

They went to work on Willis in earnest. They fell on him from all sides, all six of them dig-

53

ging at him with their fists. They threw him to the ground and someone sat on him, knocking the wind out of him.

"I've got him, I've got him." It was that fat stinking Bucky.

"Take off his pants," Rabbit said.

"Yeah, take off his pants," Sam repeated.

They were all breathing hard around him. Willis's heart swelled with dread. He thrashed around like a maniac. Only the hatred inside kept him from breaking down.

Then another voice broke into the commotion. "Halt!"

"Hey, you guys," Kinsella said, "someone's coming."

The grip on Willis's head loosened. Bucky scrambled off him. They all jumped away, looking around. Willis got to his feet, straightening his clothes. Looking up to the top of the hill, he saw that his rescuer was Richard Hayfoot. He must have climbed up from the other side and seen them. Now he stood up there like a giant scarecrow, waving his arms and yelling, "Halt. Halt. Halt."

"Look who got you scared," Bucky jeered at Kinsella. "It's Pierce's nursemaid, Pierce's retard nursemaid."

"Retard nursemaid," Larry Dodge echoed.

THE WAR ON VILLA STREET

He started jumping around, imitating Richard's flapping arms.

"Come on, forget that moron!" Rabbit said.

But just then Richard lost his balance, his feet flew out from under him, and he came sliding down the cliff on the seat of his pants. The boys laughed and applauded, and in all the confusion Willis got away. He crossed the street and no one stopped him. He could have gotten completely away then, but he didn't want to leave without his jacket. Keeping his eye on Rabbit and a good distance between himself and the Avengers, he waited to see what would happen.

Across the street Richard had landed, spitting and coughing. His glasses were askew. Saliva dripped from his mouth. "The nut's gone crazy," one of the redheads said. Someone laughed uneasily, and everyone backed away from the tall boy.

Richard had hurt his arm. He hopped around, cradling his elbow and moaning.

"He's foaming at the mouth," Sam said.

"Rabies!" Phil Dodge jumped as Richard came near him. "Hey, let's get out of here before he bites someone."

The Dodge twins were the first to go, but the others followed quickly. They were really afraid

55

of Richard, so they'd forgotten all about Willis. But Rabbit remembered. Looking across the street, he shouted, "You still owe me, Pierce. Next time!"

When they were gone, Willis crossed the street again. He tucked his shirt into his pants and slowly smoothed back his hair. A blister was forming inside his lip.

"Willis Pierce, saved your life," Richard said excitedly. His glasses were still sideways on his face. He was covered with dust. "Saved your life," he bellowed. "Saved your life."

Willis's face burned. He remembered Bucky's shout. *Pierce's retard nursemaid.* It filled Willis with self-disgust to realize that, in a way, Richard was right. If he hadn't come along and made all that noise, there was no telling what Rabbit and company would have done to him. He could still feel their hands on him, holding him helpless on the ground and yanking at his pants.

Forget it, he told himself. *Six on one, that's the way they got you.* Six on one. All bigger than him. Every one of them fatter, heavier, taller than he was. But even saying that couldn't lessen the painful sense of humiliation he felt. What kind of person was he, having to be rescued by a retard? By half a human being?

He looked up at his jacket caught on the tree. He started climbing the cliff toward it. Richard watched from below, making enthusiastic climbing motions in the air. "Go on home," Willis yelled as he shook his jacket loose. But Richard didn't go, and as the jacket floated to the ground he held out his arms and caught it.

Willis scrambled down the hill. He took the jacket from Richard and brushed it off. A rip down one side of the pocket made him feel sick. It was almost worse than the beating. Right in front, too, where it couldn't be missed. Maybe he could sew it up so his mother wouldn't know.

As he started for home, Richard dogged his heels, talking about his "rescue" of Willis, until Willis turned on him. "I don't want to hear any more about it!"

Richard grinned uneasily. "Okay, Willis, I gotcha. I gotcha!"

Finally, at the corner of Fairfield Street, Richard turned off. Fairfield was on the other side of East Broadway, not that far from Villa Street, but a lot nicer. The houses were all a little bit bigger, set farther back from the sidewalk, and had enclosed porches, and cupolas, and bigger, greener lawns. There weren't any apartment houses on Fairfield.

"I live down there, right down there in that yellow house," Richard said. "I live there with Poppy and Gramma."

Willis didn't reply. "Good-bye, Willis Pierce," Richard yelled behind him. Willis just kept moving along.

When he got home he was surprised to find both his parents home. "Where were you?" his mother said, coming out of her bedroom. She wore jeans and her fluffy pink slippers.

"No place." He didn't feel like talking. He wanted to be left alone. Passing his parents' bedroom he saw his father resting on the bed, his eyes closed.

"What have you been doing?" his mother said, following him.

"Nothing." He kept his face averted.

"You taking care of your new jacket? Let's see it."

He slid past her. "It's all right, Mom. You don't have to look at it every five minutes."

He stepped into his room and hung the jacket in the back of the closet, then just stood there. He didn't want his mother to know he'd been in a fight. "Don't you have to go to work, Mom?"

"I took off tonight," she said. "Your father's home, did you notice? And it's Friday night. *Comprenez?*"

"Sure, Mom." He got it. No boozing tonight. After she left, he took a clean shirt from the closet. He felt washed out, slow and heavy, and depressed. His mother had looked so hopeful, just like she didn't know how many times before his father had made the same promise.

Willis felt sorry for his mother. He really loved her, and it made him feel rotten to see the way she was getting up her hopes about his father. What for? So they could be knocked down? The way Rabbit and Bucky and the others had knocked him down and pushed his face into the dirt? That was what happened when you got up your hopes. No, thanks. Not for him.

CHAPTER 6

Standing in front of the mirror, Willis examined his lip. It had healed fast over the weekend, so the evidence of his beating by the Rabbit gang was gone. What remained with him was not the physical hurt, but the humiliation. He'd never forget the raging helpless feeling when they'd pinned him to the ground. He knew he had to do something about it. Tell them off at least. Maybe it wasn't much, but it was better than keeping silent.

In the privacy of his bedroom he had crudely

sewed up the rip in his jacket. He kept his hand over the lumpy seam when he walked past his mother.

At noon he stood uneasily on the landing leading down to the crowded cafeteria. The red Field Day posters were tacked up everywhere. They were all over the school. Willis looked across the room to Rabbit's regular table, a choice spot against the wall that commanded a view of the entire cafeteria. If a table "belonged" to a certain kid like Rabbit you sat there at your own risk. Willis, and other kids like him, would just sit wherever they could.

He walked toward Rabbit's table. He saw Kinsella's long sleek blond head, and Bucky's fat face. Sam and redheaded Larry Dodge were there, too. Threading his way across the room, he nervously zipped his mended jacket up and down. He felt as if everyone were looking at him, but he couldn't turn back. He'd made up his mind. He didn't know what he was going to say, but he was going to say something.

They all looked up as he approached the table. Bucky was shoveling in the chipped-beef-and-rice special. Bits of rice were plastered on his lower lip. "You ruined my jacket," Willis said. He hated the shaky way his voice sounded. "Who's paying for my new jacket?"

Bucky paused in his chewing. "You guys hear anything? I think I hear a mosquito."

"*Bzzzz*," Kinsella said obligingly.

Bucky slapped the table hard. "Got it!"

They were all so cool and superior. "Who's going to pay?" Willis repeated, pointing to the rip. "This jacket cost plenty."

"Look, fella, what do you want *me* to do?" Bucky said, holding out his empty hand in mock sincerity. "I'm flat."

"Me, too," Sam said.

"Cross my heart." Kinsella put his hand over his track jersey number.

Dodge just sat there and giggled.

"We'd like to help," Bucky said. "We really would. Why don't we take up a collection, guys?" He opened the empty milk carton in front of him. "Who wants to contribute?"

"Here's mine," Kinsella said, balling his sandwich wrapper.

"Mine!" Sam aimed an apple core at the carton.

"And mine," Bucky said, spitting into the carton. He grabbed Willis's arm. "Listen, you, Rabbit ain't paying you for any fucking jacket. He's going to be coming around for contributions to his own fund any time now. You better be ready!"

Willis's heart was pounding. Bucky's fat

hand on his arm made him feel sick. He shook free and walked away, but seated himself near enough so they could see him and he could see them. He hated them. He'd hound them. He'd never leave them alone. Every time they looked up, he'd be watching them, waiting for them to pay up. They owed him! But it was such a stupid little hope. He knew he'd never get a dime out of them. He opened his lunch bag, then pushed it aside. He wasn't hungry.

"Willis, Willis." Richard Hayfoot came toward him, holding his tray of food against his chest. "How you doing, Willis? Hi! I saw you right away." He sat down next to Willis.

Willis got up and moved to another table. Richard followed, hardly interrupting the flow of words. "You like it better here? Me, too." He talked and talked. Did he ever stop talking? Did he ever stop smiling? Or drooling and spitting? Willis looked around uneasily. Richard's loud voice probably carried to every corner of the cafeteria.

"I got a bad report today, Willis, it's all Tommy Lee's fault, he's always bothering me for my paper, and then Miss Herman gets mad at me. I do good work, but she gets real mad at me."

Willis glanced at the clock, then over at the gang again. Richard looked up, too, then down worriedly at his wristwatch. "Is it time yet? I want to be in class on time. This afternoon we have gym, we're going to practice basketball. Poppy says, 'Keep shooting those baskets, Richard. Practice hard every day. Keep trying.' I have to try harder than anybody." He bent to carefully knot the laces on his sneakers. Then he launched into a long story about living with his "Poppy" and his "Gramma." "My mommy died when I was a little baby, a little baby just born." His face saddened. "I never saw her. You want to see her picture?"

"No," Willis said.

But Richard was already digging out his wallet. Willis noticed that it was real leather and looked expensive. Richard had money in his wallet, too, which surprised Willis. "Isn't she pretty? That's my mommy." He had a picture in laminated plastic of a young woman sitting on the steps of a house. He kissed the picture. "Miss Herman says she's pretty. Do you think she's pretty, Willis?" Carefully, he put the picture away. "I'm lucky because I have my Gramma. Gramma says, 'Play on the porch when it's raining, don't get all wet and catch a cold.' Crazy old woman! She wants me to come right home after school when I'm coughing." He coughed in Willis's direction.

Willis had had as much as he could take. He got up and walked out of the lunchroom. But Richard followed him and caught up with him in the hall. "Is it time to go, Willis?"

"Yeah, *go*. Scram! Go on back to your friends in the lunchroom. Your friend Bucky is calling."

Richard shook his head. "Bucky's not my friend. You're my friend, Willis Pierce, because I saved you. I told Poppy and he was really happy. He said he saved somebody in the war a long time ago, and that made them friends forever. Just like us, friends forever."

Willis dug his hands into his pockets. "Look, Richard—" He spoke in a slow, loud voice so the retard would get it. "I don't have any friends. And if I did, you'd be at the bottom of the bottom of the list. Okay?"

There was a confused expression on Richard's face. "But, Willis, Poppy said—" Then a smile. "Oh! You're kidding me. Now I get it, now I get it. You're kidding me. Poppy and me kid, too. I get it."

Willis raised his eyes in frustration. Sue Tyson was standing nearby on the other side of the glass trophy case, drumming on the glass with her fingers. She must have heard everything. She had that know-it-all expression on her face. Willis pushed Richard aside and ran down the hall. Sometimes he felt like all he had was bad luck. Why did it have to be Sue Tyson who heard Richard blabbing about "saving" him? Now she'd turn around and tell Marion, he was sure of it. And then they'd laugh together, at him. All afternoon he couldn't get that thought out of his mind.

When he left school Richard was holding the outside door open, giving every kid a big goofy smile and a loud "Have a nice day!" But as soon as Willis appeared he let go of the door and fell into step with him. "Want a piece of chocolate?" He held out a candy bar.

"No!" Willis walked faster. Richard kept up with him. Willis broke into a trot to warm up for his run.

"Where you going so fast?" Richard panted.

"I run every day," Willis said curtly. It was a relief when he left Richard behind.

All week Richard continued to pursue Willis. He was like some huge annoying insect buzzing around Willis's head. He had got it firmly fixed in his mind that he and Willis were best friends, and nothing Willis said could shake that conviction. "Bug off, bug off!" Willis yelled one day. Richard smiled uneasily, but in a moment he had bounced back like a rubber ball.

Willis began to despair of ever getting rid of

the overgrown leech, short of pounding him to a pulp. Well, he wasn't about to do that. It would be too much like beating up on a little kid. Every day Richard waited for him and walked the few blocks with him till Willis began his run. Willis decided his best bet was just to ignore Richard. Easier said than done. For one thing, Richard never stopped talking, and then sometimes the things he said were so dopey Willis couldn't help reacting.

"I'm six feet, and I'm still growing, Willis. It's heraldy. Poppy says it's heraldy that makes us two so big. Heraldy is why we're the way we are. You got little heraldy, I got big heraldy."

"You mean *heredity*," Willis said, despite himself. And then, with what had become an automatic gesture, he checked out the street to see if Rabbit's gang was anywhere around. He and Richard were on East Broadway, a street of gas stations, houses, and stores. A busy street with an endless stream of cars. Willis kicked aside a dented beer can. He hadn't forgotten about Rabbit. He was on the alert all the time, on the street and in school, both.

His little dream of hounding Rabbit had fizzled. Instead, when he saw Bucky and Sam cruising the corridors in school he reversed direction to avoid them. But he still had thoughts about revenging himself on Rabbit someday, somehow.

"In May it's my birthday, Willis. May twenty-two, I'll be sixteen years old. What do you think I should ask for, for my birthday?"

"How should I know?"

"I gotta think about it. I gotta ask for good stuff. Poppy says, 'Better come up with some good ideas, Richard!'"

"You're too old for presents," Willis said shortly.

"Don't big boys get presents? Not even one present? That would be all right, wouldn't it, Willis? I'll tell Poppy. Poppy says presents are nice."

"Poppy says . . . Poppy says . . ." Richard couldn't talk for two minutes without bringing in his father. "Poppy" used to be a champion basketball player. "Poppy" worked in Citibank. "Poppy" knew everything about money. To listen to Richard, "Poppy" knew everything there was to know about everything. If "Poppy" told him to jump off a bridge, Willis had no doubt he'd do it.

It really irritated Willis to hear Richard talking about his father like he was some kind of combination of Abe Lincoln, General Mac-Arthur, and God. Every time, he couldn't help thinking of his own father. What could his "Poppy" do? Drink. Period. No, that was unfair. He could do other things. He could weld. He could shoot, he could fix machines. He could do plenty, but all the same Willis wouldn't go around boasting about him.

"Poppy gives Gramma presents all the time," Richard was saying. "Birthday presents, Christmas presents, everything. He's nice, Willis. He gives Christmas presents to all the people in the bank, and to Mr. Jeffrey in the barbershop. And Mr. Jeffrey gives me candy every time we go in to see him. Every time, Willis, even if I don't get a haircut. He's a very nice man."

Nice. Willis hated that word. It was such a lie. People weren't nice. Maybe your own family was okay, but that was all. Everyone else was out for what he could get. Dog eat dog. Richard's dumb face, so full of sincerity and belief in "nice" people and his "nice Poppy," disgusted Willis. He felt like kicking the big dope in his big soft ass. It was crazy, but he really wanted to hurt him, show him, pound that nice-Poppy nice-people stuff right out of him.

"People stink," he said.

"No, Willis, don't say that."

Willis gripped Richard's arm. "People stink," he repeated. He noticed a group of girls ahead of them looking into a store window. And at the same moment he saw a sodden cigar butt in the gutter. "See this?" he said, snatching up the butt. "See this dirty thing? Now watch me," he said to Richard. "I'm going to show you how nice people are." He ran up to the girls and shoved the cigar butt down the collar of the nearest girl. As he did it he saw that it was Marion Bouchard.

Marion turned. Her cool calm eyes went wide. Willis stepped back, so startled he felt the breath drain out of his body. Marion yanked up her blouse, showing smooth skin and the bottom of her bra. The soggy brown cigar butt dropped to the ground.

Susan Tyson, who was there, too, toed the cigar butt into the gutter. "You filthy baby," she said to Willis, "why don't you grow up?"

Willis couldn't speak. Words formed at the back of his tongue, but he couldn't push them past his stiff lips. It was a mistake. He hadn't meant to— Not to Marion! *I was just going to show Richard . . . I didn't mean . . . I'm sorry. . . .*

Marion stared at him in disgust, then with Susan and her other friends protectively around her she walked off. Willis stood there miserably. Why had he done such a terrible thing? Why hadn't he realized it was Marion? Why hadn't he looked first? He took a few steps after Marion, but then stopped. Even if he could find the words to explain, she'd never believe him. She'd never believe anything he said.

"Was that Marion Bouchard?" Richard said, coming up to him. "She's pretty. Why did you put that cigar butt down her blouse, Willis? Don't you like her?"

Willis stared at him for a moment, then turned and ran the other way.

CHAPTER 7

"Don't go 'way," Willis's father said. He was in his underwear, his feet bare, face wrinkled with sleep. "I'm going to sleep a little more. We do something later." He shuffled past to his bedroom.

It was Saturday morning. The night before he'd come home from work. Still not drinking. Two weeks. Time for Willis to start crossing his fingers? No, not yet; his father had managed to stay off booze for two weeks other times. Once he'd done it for almost a month.

THE WAR ON VILLA STREET

After his mother left for work, Willis turned on the TV in the living room and watched cartoons for a while. In the bedroom the bed creaked and his father muttered in his sleep. "Pop?" Willis said hopefully. It was a sunny day and he was eager to get out.

Off and on his father got this urge to do things with Willis. A few times they'd gone rat hunting at the dump. Once his father had taken him shopping for school clothes. Another time the three of them had gone to the zoo. Maybe today they'd go to a ball game in MacArthur Stadium and then eat out at Danzer's, or Aunt Josie's, where you could get some of the best pizza in the city. One thing about his father, he was no tightwad. When he had money he didn't mind spending it.

Willis yawned. He had spent an uneasy night, waking often to remember the awful, stupid thing he had done to Marion. Over and over he had asked himself, *Why did it have to be Marion?* But there was no answer. Just bad luck.

He stood by the window, looking down. On the street a tall bald man passed arm in arm with a fat boy Willis knew from school. "Hey, Rosenballoon," Willis called. But they were too far away. The man was wearing jeans and sneakers. Sneakers! Willis's father never wore sneakers. When he was sober and feeling good he could dress up to make every other man in sight look sick. Jacket, tie, hat, and shining leather brogues. His father was a nut about shoes. He had five pairs lined up in his closet. And he made a real production shining them. He'd spread newspapers on the kitchen floor and go to work with paste polish, rags, and brushes. When his father was done you could see your face in his shoes.

The morning passed slowly. Several times Willis stood in the bedroom doorway. "You getting up soon, Pop?" His father, head buried under the pillow, didn't move. Willis yawned and for the tenth time went into the kitchen to look at the clock.

At last he heard his father shuffling heavily through the apartment. "Louise? Louise?" Willis took a last bite of the sandwich he'd made for himself, then hopped off the windowsill.

His father appeared. "Why didn't you answer me when I call?"

"You were calling Mom." What a grouch.

"And you stand there like a jackass and say nothing!"

Willis's face turned rigid. Was this what he'd waited for all morning? He turned away

THE WAR ON VILLA STREET

to hide the sudden lump of emotion rising in his throat. His father went into the bathroom. Willis grabbed his jacket. "I'm going out," he shouted, and without waiting for an answer he slammed the door behind him.

The moment he hit the street he started running. He ran for a long time till he got the heat out of his gut. By then he was thinking that he ought to have realized staying off the booze could make his father irritable and tense as a hot wire. But he still didn't want to go home.

He circled over to the Prescott Street playground. On one of the black Tarvia courts Bucky and Sam were playing around with Richard Hayfoot. His first impulse was to back off, then he stood his ground. He wasn't afraid of them, not without Rabbit and the rest of the little Mafia to back them up.

"Here, Richard." Sam feinted the ball toward Richard, who eagerly held up his hands. Sam threw the ball to Bucky, and the two of them laughed as Richard rushed futilely between them.

"It's my ball. My turn. Please give me my ball, Bucky."

At the fence Willis watched scornfully. Taking the ball away from Richard was like taking candy from a baby.

75

"What are you looking at?" Bucky said, noticing him.

"Nothing worth seeing," Willis said. "What's the matter, can't find anybody your own size to play with?"

"Bigmouth," Bucky said, then shouted, "Look out! Rabbit's behind you!"

Before he could stop himself Willis jerked around. Bucky and Sam laughed hysterically. A wave of heat went through Willis. How often was he going to let them make a fool of him? He ached to turn things around and settle scores. An idea came to him. "I'll take on the two of you," he said, swaggering onto the court.

"You against us?"

"Sure." He'd run rings around them.

Bucky and Sam exchanged glances. Then Bucky smiled in his sly way. "Oh, no, that wouldn't be fair," he said piously. "Tell you what. Me and Sam against you and Richard."

Willis's throat tightened. He controlled his anger and disgust. They were trying to make a fool of him again, lumping him with Richard. But if he walked out now, they'd call him chicken, have something else on him. "You're on," he said. He could still run rings around them, Richard or no Richard.

He took the ball from Richard, barely glancing at the big dummy's eager face. He charged toward the basket, elbowing Bucky aside. He leaped, threw, and made the basket.

"Foul," Sam said. "We weren't ready."

"You going to cry every time I make a basket?"

Looking sullen, Sam took the ball, bounced it, then shot it to Bucky who threw it back to Sam. Willis intercepted. Another basket.

"Hey, hey, hey," Richard applauded. "You did it, Willis, right through the hole-y hole."

Sam and Bucky weren't laughing now. They started crowding Willis, leaping in front of him so he couldn't get off a shot. He stopped, bounced the ball.

"Shoot!" Bucky ordered. "Play ball."

Willis feinted left, then pivoted to the right, letting the ball go in a pretty arc over their outstretched fingers. The ball hit the rim, hovered a moment, then fell in.

"Lucky shot," Sam muttered, but a moment later when he tried a jump shot he missed the basket completely.

"What's the matter?" Willis said. "Can't find the basket without Rabbit holding your hand?"

He had them mad and straining. They wanted to kill him, but they couldn't do it playing basketball. "Give your partner the ball,"

Harry Mazer

they yelled. "You're hogging the ball." They figured playing with Richard would throw him off.

Shrugging, Willis got into a huddle with Richard. "I'm going to pass you the ball," he said, "but when I yell, you throw it back to me. Got that?"

Richard nodded eagerly. "Gotcha! Gotcha!" Willis had his doubts about Richard, but surprisingly his strategy worked. Richard had the ball, Bucky and Sam charged him, Willis yelled, and Richard threw wildly. Luckily, Willis retrieved and made another basket. Ten points, and Bucky and Sam were still skunked. A real shutout.

Willis relaxed and began to enjoy himself. The taunts from Bucky and Sam were sweet music to him now. "Stay on Sam," he told Richard. "Don't let him shoot." But Richard had trouble keeping up with Sam, and he was easily fooled. Still, he was dogged. He ran after Sam, lunging into him, waving his arms around, and generally bothering Sam enough to throw off his shot. Amazingly, he snagged the rebound.

"I got it, I got it," he cried. He leaped into the air, and in his joy threw the ball so hard

78

it soared over the backboard and out of the court.

"You idiot," Bucky said. "Go get it. Go on, shag it."

When Richard came back with the ball, Sam held out his hands. "Throw it here."

But Willis had other ideas. "I've had enough," he said. "Keep the ball, Richard."

Bucky shoved up aggressively against Willis. "What do you mean, you've had enough? We're playing a game. You can't quit."

"You guys bore me." Willis yawned. "No competition."

Bucky's face darkened. "Don't give me that shit." He snapped his fingers at Richard. "Pass that ball here."

Richard looked uncertainly to Willis. "It's my ball. I don't have to give it to you. Isn't that right, Willis?"

"Right," Willis said. Richard clutched his ball more firmly. Bucky looked like he was going to have a fit. He was used to everyone jumping when he snapped his fingers. But Willis was in control now, and enjoying every moment.

"Toss the ball here, Richard," he said, showing off his power. He caught the ball and bounced it coolly.

Harry Mazer

"Let's play," Sam whined. "What's holding things up?"

"I told you, you guys bore me." Nice of Sam to give him the chance to rub it in. "Anyway, I thought of something more interesting to do."

"What's that, pick your toenails?" Bucky sneered.

Willis bounced the ball on the foul line. "I'm going to give Richard a basketball clinic. I figure of the three of you, he's the most promising." He tossed the ball to Richard. "Let's see you shoot, Richard."

Standing flat-footed, Richard threw the ball with a funny upward movement of his arms. The ball sailed high, but nowhere near the basket.

"Know why the retard missed?" Bucky said loudly. "Because he's got a retard teacher. Hey, little retard. Rabbit's coming!"

Willis laughed out loud, untouchable for the moment. "Don't let those guys worry you," he told Richard. "You just think about the ball. Always keep your eye on the ball." He passed the ball to Richard, instructing him on dribbling.

Although he'd started the "clinic" just to get under Bucky's skin, Willis got involved in actually trying to teach Richard. It wasn't easy,

80

although Richard, tongue clamped between his teeth, tried so hard to do what Willis wanted that sweat burst out on his forehead. "Is that right, Willis? Is that right?"

"Try again. Straighten up when you dribble, and bounce the ball higher."

When he looked around, Bucky and Sam were gone. Sneaked away, Willis thought scornfully, like dogs with their tails between their legs. He was pleased by the thought. Not that whipping them at a single game of basketball could make up for what they'd done to him.

"Richard." A tall heavy man with a handlebar mustache was leaning against the fence.

"That's my Poppy," Richard exclaimed. He ran to his father. Willis wondered how long Mr. Hayfoot had been watching.

"Having a good time?" Mr. Hayfoot loosened Richard's collar. He nodded to Willis. "Hello."

"Hello," Willis said, smoothing back his hair. He studied Richard's father. So this was the great Poppy, the man who knew everything and could do anything. He didn't look so special to Willis. He was wearing jeans and a broad-striped shirt just like anybody.

"Poppy, this is my best friend, this is Willis Pierce. He's teaching me to play basketball. This is my friend."

"See you," Willis said, handing the ball to Richard. That best-friend shit really irritated him.

"Wait a minute," Richard's father said. "Don't run away. Willis—is that the name?" Willis, turning, nodded reluctantly. "Got a minute, Willis? Let's play a little ball. I like to fool around." He gave Willis a high-powered smile. "I was watching you before. You're good." He took the ball from Richard.

Willis shrugged and caught the ball neatly as Mr. Hayfoot flipped it to him.

"Okay, boys, let's go," Richard's father said.

Willis moved in toward the basket, but Mr. Hayfoot, towering over him, didn't make it easy. Willis decided to try a feint, then a quick throw. Mr. Hayfoot intercepted, then dunked the ball into the basket. He was at least six foot two, maybe three. Not exactly an evenly matched game, but Willis enjoyed it. He played hard and ran Mr. Hayfoot's ass off.

The only problem was, Mr. Hayfoot kept giving the ball to Richard and telling him to lay it up. Richard flubbed, no surprise, but his father praised him anyway. "Good boy! Good try!"

They played till Mr. Hayfoot, the sweat running down his cheeks, called a halt. "I've had it, boys." He wiped his face on his T-shirt. Long before, he'd thrown off his shirt.

"Richard says you played basketball in college, Mr. Hayfoot," Willis said.

"That's right." Mr. Hayfoot smoothed his mustache. "What else did he say?"

"That you work in Citibank."

"He's the president, he's the president of everything," Richard shouted.

Mr. Hayfoot put his finger to his mouth. "Shh. Calm down, Richard. You just promoted me. *Vice*-president, you know that. And just one of seven."

"The vice-president, Willis. He's the vice-president."

"How come you live over here?" Willis said. "You must be rich." Why'd he say that? He'd stuck his foot into his mouth that time.

But Mr. Hayfoot didn't seem mad. "I like it around here, Willis. It's where I grew up. I want Richard to grow up the way I did. Right, Richie?" He clapped Richard on the shoulder. "Well, how about a cold drink?"

"I'm dying for a cold drink," Richard said.

Mr. Hayfoot gave Richard a dollar and told him to go across to Nedman's and buy three thirty-cent drinks. He spoke in an ordinary way to Richard, but slowly and emphatically. "How much change will you have coming, Richard?"

"Three thirties," Richard said, hopping around. "Thirty, thirty, and thirty—" He was

83

figuring in his hand. His lips formed the word *ninety.* He looked hopefully at his father.

"I don't want anything to drink," Willis interrupted. "I've got to go now." He'd hung around too long as it was. He wasn't Richard's buddy, and the whole crazy situation was getting on his nerves. If he wanted a cold drink he could have it at home.

"Hey, hold on, will you, fella?" Mr. Hayfoot said, putting his hand lightly on Willis's shoulder. "I want to talk to you. Okay, Richie, off you go."

"'Bye, Poppy. 'Bye, Willis. I'll be right back." Richard dogtrotted to the gate.

What did Mr. Hayfoot have to say to him? Willis wondered uneasily. Suddenly it occurred to him that Mr. Hayfoot knew about his father's drinking. Mr. Hayfoot was an important man, he would know stuff like that about people who lived around here. Maybe he felt sorry for Willis, and that was why he put on this big buddy-buddy act. Well, let him feel sorry for *himself* with his weirdo retarded son! Willis stood very straight, his hands dug into his pockets.

"Willis"—Mr. Hayfoot smoothed both ends of his mustache—"I want to ask you something. What do you think of Richard?"

"Richard?" Willis looked down at his sneakers. He hadn't expected that question. What was he supposed to say? What a dumb question. He knew for sure Mr. Hayfoot didn't want to hear what he really thought about Richard. "He's all right," he said.

"Yeah, he's a nice guy," Mr. Hayfoot said. "But what do you think about the way he learns? He picks up things, doesn't he? I'm really interested in your evaluation of him."

Willis kicked at the Tarvia. He wasn't going to tell Mr. Hayfoot his own son was a dope. Not that Richard was so bad if you thought about him like a real little kid. Just pretend some shrimpy kindergarten squirt was hiding inside that drooling, smiling, talky, six-foot clown. "Richard's okay."

"I can see that he trusts you." Mr. Hayfoot had blue eyes just like Richard's. It was weird because they really looked a lot alike, but Richard was a retard and his father was a vice-president of a bank. Willis wondered how such nutty things happened. Maybe there were other retards in the Hayfoot family. There was nothing wrong with the brains in his own family, he thought, stiffening with pride.

"Richard feels you're his friend," Mr. Hayfoot said.

"No," Willis said plainly. "I'm not his friend. I just see him around sometimes."

"You were helping him. Showing him how

to shoot baskets." Mr. Hayfoot tapped him on the shoulder. "Most people don't even do that. If they did, Richard would be a lot farther along."

"Along where?" Willis said. He kept wondering what all this was leading up to.

"Along the road to being like other boys," Mr. Hayfoot said. "Richard is retarded, but he's a borderline case. He can learn. And the more attention he gets, the more he can learn. Did you notice the way he started shooting better after we both worked out with him?"

Not really, Willis thought. He bounced the ball. He wished Mr. Hayfoot would get to the point. He didn't think for a moment that Mr. Hayfoot was just passing the time of day.

"You know, Willis," Mr. Hayfoot said, "Richard doesn't have a mother. He has only me and his grandmother. Now, his grandmother babies him a bit, but he needs the love and attention she gives him. It's important, especially for a boy like Richard. And I do the best I can for him, but there are many, many hours in the day when no one is really working with him, teaching him things. Last summer I had a boy working with him, but he was no good."

Willis shifted. Mr. Hayfoot was looking right at him. All this talk, the confidential air, Mr.

Hayfoot's tone of utmost seriousness impressed Willis. Shit, this must be the way Mr. Hayfoot talked to the other six vice-presidents!

"I've given a lot of thought to this, Willis. I was watching you today, and I was impressed. You have ability, athletic ability. I like the way you move, I like your ease and coordination. I think it's important for Richard to be around people like you. He learns by imitation and contact. He could learn a great deal from you."

Willis didn't say anything. Now he could see where all this was leading, and he was kicking himself for ever going on the court with Richard. Mr. Hayfoot wanted to nail him down as a "friend" of Richard's. Willis rocked back on his heels. Poor old Richard. Even if he was a retard, it couldn't be much fun having his father running around getting friends for him.

"I want Richard to participate in the Field Day your school is going to have in May. Last year he didn't take part, and I think it was a mistake. I don't want him left out of the normal events of a boy's life. You understand, Willis? Taking part in things is important for his feeling about himself. The more he does, the more confidence he should have. And he needs confidence very badly. Now, I think a normal, well-coordinated, confident boy like you can do a lot for him. Someday I hope he'll be able to hold down a job and live a semblance of a normal life. What I'd want you to do, Willis, is coach Richard, with Field Day in mind. Getting him prepared for Field Day would be the immediate goal."

Coach Richard! The very idea of having anything to do with Richard on a regular basis appalled Willis. Richard was a retard. A queer, an alien, an outsider. From another planet. Willis was in enough trouble by himself. The last thing in the world that he needed was some dopey space cadet like Richard hanging on to his shirt.

"I'm not interested," he said flatly.

"It would be strictly business," Mr. Hayfoot said. "Three dollars an hour for every hour you spend with Richie after school. Weekends, too. Whatever time you log, I'll pay you."

Willis stared at Mr. Hayfoot. Had he heard right? Three dollars an hour? Crazy. He flipped the ball into the air, forced to consider what Mr. Hayfoot was saying.

"I'd want you to concentrate on his physical skills, naturally. Running and jumping. His coordination and timing. Schoolwork we'll leave to Miss Herman. You were teaching him basketball today. It could be baseball tomorrow, or handball. There's a lot you can do. No end to the things, and it would mean a lot to Richard. And to me." Mr. Hayfoot looked seriously and expectantly at Willis. "Of course if you don't want to do it, I'll try to find someone else."

Willis walked away, bouncing the ball. He liked the money part, liked it a lot. How could he help it? Three dollars an hour was nothing to sneeze at. If he took on Richard a couple hours every school day, plus a few hours on the weekends, that could mean thirty-five, forty dollars a week. In a month a hundred and sixty dollars. Maybe even as much as two hundred a month. Willis whistled slowly. A lot of money. Tempting, awfully tempting.

If he took the job he could give his mother money every week. Then she wouldn't have to beg his father. She'd be more independent, they'd both be a lot freer. All right, his father was on the wagon now. Two big weeks. Sure, and the way he'd been acting that morning it didn't look like he'd hold out another two days.

He could see himself handing money over to his mother. *Here you are, Mom.* She'd smile, she'd hug him. And it wouldn't have to matter so much to her what his father did.

"How much?" He wanted to hear Mr. Hayfoot say it again. Grown-ups could tell you one thing today, and something else the next.

"Three dollars an hour. Want me to put it in writing?"

Willis nodded. "Okay."

Mr. Hayfoot took a pad out of his pocket and wrote on it. He tore off the sheet of paper and handed it to Willis.

"I will pay Willis Pierce $3 per hour for each hour he spends with my son, Richard Hayfoot, improving his physical skills." And he'd signed it in an important-looking scrawl, "M. John Hayfoot."

Willis read it over twice. Three dollars an hour. There it was in writing. And Mr. Hayfoot's signature.

"Is it a deal?" Mr. Hayfoot said. "Let's shake on it." He put out his hand. Willis hesitated. Then he thought of his father again, bleary-eyed and nasty this morning. His stomach tightened. He took Mr. Hayfoot's hand. They shook.

"Great!" Mr. Hayfoot clapped him on the back. And at the same moment Willis saw Richard coming toward them, his mouth hanging open, the three cans of soda hugged against his chest. Willis's heart sank. It had all happened too fast. What had he let himself in for?

CHAPTER 8

Monday after school Willis went downstairs to the basement where the Special Ed class had its homeroom. Sauntering through the dim corridor, he tried to appear nonchalant. He leaned against the wall some distance from Miss Herman's room and folded his arms.

The corridor was filling with Special Ed kids pushing and shoving toward the lockers and stairs. Miss Herman stood in the open door of her room, slowing the kids down. She wore a brown-and-beige suit, glasses, and a long rope of glass beads. She was half the size of some of the kids shoving out of her room.

Willis didn't know why, but looking at those kids upset him. Even the ones that looked normal. He was really annoyed with himself for being here. It had been dumb to agree to pick Richard up at his classroom. A group of girls rushed past, and Willis made his face blank as they glanced at him. He didn't want anyone to guess that he was waiting for someone from the Special class.

Starting tomorrow he'd meet Richard at the parkway, near the footbridge that ran over the highway and across to the creek. You could run for miles along the creek and probably not meet anyone you knew. No way was he going to be seen with Richard on the playground or in their neighborhood. Their connection was strictly business. Richard was a job he'd taken for the money, and he didn't want anyone drawing any other conclusions. In the back of his mind he was uneasily aware that Richard wouldn't have the same reservations. Somehow, he'd have to deal with Richard's big mouth.

"Don't get in any fights, Perry," Miss Herman warned a tall boy with wild hair. And to a really pretty girl with dark hair, she said, "Beth Marie, tell your sister you have to come to school every day."

The lower corridor emptied rapidly. Still no Richard. Miss Herman disappeared around the corner. After a moment Willis crossed the hall and stepped into the classroom. The room was empty. He looked around curiously. Desks clumped together, words written on the blackboard. "It is the month of March. A windy month." High ceilings, and long barred windows like all the rooms in the old building.

"Can I help you with something?" Miss Herman stood in the doorway, regarding him coolly through tinted glasses. Willis could smell the cigarette she'd just been smoking. "Are you looking for someone?"

"Ri—" he started to say, but clamped his mouth shut. He started to walk out.

"Hold it right there, buster." She opened the bottom drawer of her desk, took out her purse, and checked its contents.

Willis stood there, red-faced and humiliated. She snapped her pocketbook shut. "Can I go now?" He made his voice as cold and sarcastic as possible. She gave him a long unblinking stare, then dismissed him with a wave of her hand.

He stamped up the stairs. She didn't know

him, she didn't know who he was, or what he was like, but she had her mind made up the minute she saw him that he was a thief. He hated people like that. He'd met them before. Landlords of houses where they'd lived, and grocers, and the manager of the variety store on South Avenue. People who looked at you with cold suspicious eyes and always thought the worst.

Outside, Willis looked up and down the street. Track-team boys and girls, yellow shorts over their gray sweat pants, streamed out from the gym in separate packs and crossed the street to the field. He saw Kinsella and Larry Dodge. Mr. Weber, holding a clipboard, blew his whistle.

"Over here," the coach called. "On the double." The kids all turned and ran toward him.

Bunch of robots. Willis could have been on the track team, but he wasn't interested in being anybody's little tin soldier. If he felt like running, he ran. And if, like now, he felt like standing around with his hands in his pockets, he did that.

But actually he felt at loose ends. He had been primed to start working out with Richard. He had thought of little else since Saturday afternoon, making his plans on how he'd train

Richard. And now, no Richard. No teaching, and no money. In one way he was relieved. What had made him think he could suddenly turn into a teacher? He was just Willis Pierce, just an ordinary kid. He'd let himself be sucked in by the big money Mr. Hayfoot held out. On the other hand, there'd been something about Mr. Hayfoot, his cool confidence, that had attracted Willis.

He remembered Mr. Hayfoot's high-powered smile. He was a big man, vice-president of a bank. And yet he had this dummy son and had to ask Willis Pierce to help him out. Willis turned it over in his mind, realizing another reason he had agreed to teach Richard—he had been flattered. Flattered that Mr. Hayfoot had come to him, had thought he could do something for his son. *Maybe I can. We'll see.*

Well, he'd give it a good try. He was no thief, no matter what Miss Herman or anybody else thought, and if he said he'd teach Richard for three dollars an hour, then he'd do his best to earn three dollars an hour. That was one thing he knew from his father. Sober or hung over, give a day's work for a day's pay. But still, Willis was glad he had another day before he had to start with Richard.

Hearing voices behind him, he turned, and all thoughts of Richard, and his father, and Richard's father, went flying out of his head. Marion Bouchard and Susan Tyson were coming out of the gym. Sue was carrying a red gym bag and wearing red gym shorts and sneakers. She must have been playing girls' volleyball.

Marion looked fantastic in a pleated skirt and a white pullover. Both girls were coming straight toward him. Now was the time to say something to Marion about that stupid cigar butt. To explain that it had all been a mistake. If he could only forget Sue Tyson being right there. The girls were barely two steps from him now, and Sue was looking straight at him.

"Picked up any cigar butts lately?" Sue said.

Willis flushed deeply, but stood his ground. If there was one person he couldn't stand, it was Tyson with her red gym shorts and red-and-white socks and Adidas sneakers, acting like she was some big jock. He'd like to pull those baggy gym shorts off her sometime, and then what would she do!

Forget her. He wanted to be easy and loose, to say what he meant to say only to Marion. If she would just look at him and smile, it would be so simple.

Marion, I . . . I . . . I . . .

His lips moved, but nothing came out.

THE WAR ON VILLA STREET

"Move, garbage can," Sue Tyson said. And Marion, head high, eyes sliding over him, passed him like a queen disdaining his existence.

Willis's face blazed. He followed Marion longingly with his eyes. She hated him, and it was his own fault.

The two girls turned down Columbus Avenue. Willis followed at a distance. On East Broadway they headed toward the shopping plaza. Willis wound in and out among the people on the street, far enough back so Marion wouldn't know he was following her, but not so far he would lose sight of her. He was going to speak to her. He was sure of it. Today. This afternoon. He'd smile first. Then she'd smile back. Then he'd say it. Explain about the cigar butt, how it was a big mistake, how he didn't know it was her. If he'd known, he'd never, never have done it. Never. Let Sue Tyson make all the remarks she wanted. It was the truth.

Marion and Sue turned a corner and he sped forward. They stopped for a light, and he was so close he could have tapped Marion on the shoulder.

"Pierce, hey, hi." He looked around, sure he had heard his name being called, but it was only a strange kid calling someone else. When he looked back, Marion and Sue were gone.

Harry Mazer

He ran halfway down the street before he realized they might have gone into the department store on the corner. He doubled back and entered the store. Women's stockings . . . underwear . . . the heavy fragrance of perfume . . . A woman frowned at him, and he quickly stepped back outside.

Standing on the corner he tried watching all the doors at once. *Marion. Marion. Marion.* He called her name silently. *Marion, where are you?* Trying to bring her back by repeating her name. Then he looked around the corner toward the Washington Street exit, and she was there.

He fell into step behind the two girls. They were heading back home now. He made his plans. When Sue left, he'd approach Marion and explain everything. She'd understand. They'd walk down to the park together, down where the lovers parked at night. They'd hold hands. Then he'd put his arm around her, and kiss her.

He was so deep in his fantasy that he almost lost the girls again. He ran to catch up, galloped around the corner, and almost ran into them. They were standing on the street waiting for him.

"There's Willis," Sue sang out, barely con-

THE WAR ON VILLA STREET

taining her glee. "Oh, Marion, look. It's wee
Willis Pierce."

He could have killed her. *Look her in the
eye. Show her how much you despise her.* Instead he rushed by speechlessly.

CHAPTER 9

"Hey, you!" Rabbit grabbed Willis in school. Willis broke away, but he was still cornered. Luckily there were a million other kids in the corridor. Three weeks had passed, and Willis had begun to think Rabbit had forgotten about him. But now, loud enough for half the school hear, and just as if he'd read Willis's mind, Rabbit said in a menacing tone, "Rabbit doesn't forget."

And like someone hypnotized, Willis just nodded, despising himself but unable to speak, his throat feeling as if it were jammed with wire.

"You owe me," Rabbit went on. "I got plans for you. I'm going to kick your ass good."

Past Rabbit's shoulder Willis saw Sue Tyson taking it all in, watching him acting like a zombie taking orders from his master. The blood shot to Willis's head. "And I'll kick yours," he snapped back, almost stuttering in his anger.

Rabbit's face blew up like a balloon. "You better watch it, turkey!"

Then the bell rang and Rabbit shoved past him. Why had he said anything to Rabbit? Like a fool, showing off in front of Sue Tyson. And now Rabbit had something else to chalk up against him.

He was in a bad mood when he left school. As he'd been doing for the past weeks, he met Richard at the footbridge. "Let's go," he said shortly, crossing over the parkway to the creek. Every day it didn't rain and most weekends they'd been coming here, and he'd been doing his best to prepare Richard for Field Day, which was now less than a month away. He could tell today was going to be a bad one. Five minutes, and already everything about Richard set his teeth on edge. The way Richard ambled along, that big grin on his face, his untied shoelaces, and the drool at the edge of his mouth.

Willis had a favored spot where he worked out with Richard. Alongside the creek, it was protected by a ring of trees. As usual he started Richard on calisthenics. Jumping jacks for his warm-up. "And one and two, and one and two," Willis chanted, clapping his hands over his head. "And watch me, Richard, and one and two, hands together, feet apart, that's the way," he chanted.

Saturdays Mr. Hayfoot had been showing up to watch him working with Richard, and then paying him. The first week Willis had given his mother money, she'd gone right out and bought a porterhouse steak to celebrate his new job. He liked that. The money part of the job was every bit as good as he'd thought it would be. But the Richard part of the job could drive him right up a wall.

Even though he'd known Richard was slow, Willis had still been surprised by the trouble Richard had with the simplest things. Or what Willis thought were simple things. One of his goals was for Richard to smoothly and routinely do fifty push-ups, fifty sit-ups, and twenty-five pull-ups on a tree limb. That didn't seem like too much to Willis, but nothing came easily to Richard. On the push-ups he pumped his ass instead of using his arms, he only managed to get through the sit-ups because Willis held his ankles and kept him at it, and he couldn't do more than ten pull-ups. Discouraging.

Working on the running broad jump was just as bad. After thinking over the Field Day events that Richard could take part in, Willis had decided the running broad jump was a good bet for Richard. But today he was thinking that it was really hopeless. He just couldn't get it through Richard's head or Richard's body to take off smoothly, make his run, and jump. He'd stop at the line, or he'd step over it, or if he managed to coordinate enough not to do those things, he was sure to get off on the wrong foot.

"This one is right," Willis said, barely controlling his irritation. "Right! Right! Concentrate, Richard. You have to concentrate if you want to learn."

"I like to learn," Richard said. Willis believed him. Richard listened to everything Willis said with his eyes wide with the effort to absorb. "Is this learning, Willis?"

"I've told you before, yes."

"And are you my teacher?"

"I suppose so."

"Then where are the desks?" Richard shouted gleefully. "That's a joke, Willis."

His giggling irritated Willis. He was still chewing over the encounter with Rabbit earlier that day, and Richard's silliness got on his nerves. Then and there he decided Richard would never learn the running broad jump.

He drew a new line in the dust with a stick. From now on they'd concentrate on the standing broad jump. Maybe it would be easier for Richard to jump from one place. He explained the procedure. "Stay behind the line and jump over it. Feet together, swing your arms, then jump as far as you can."

Richard nodded eagerly. "I'll do it, Willis. I'll do it."

Willis measured the jump with the new tape he'd bought. It wasn't good. Not even four feet. Richard would have to jump close to six feet before Willis would feel satisfied.

"Was that good, Willis?"

"So-so."

"I'll do better next time, Willis. Do you like me?"

Like me, like me, that was such a big deal with Richard. "*Do* like me," Willis said, "never mind 'like me.'" But Richard didn't get it.

The afternoon went on. Willis had Richard jog with him along the creek, through the park, and out to the city limits, where Richard fell down in a heap on the grass. "Too much," he panted. "I'm really tired. My legs are crying, Willis."

"Oh, knock it off, will you?" Richard had pulled this crying legs stuff on Willis before. Richard had his act down pat. He could really lay it on when he wanted to get out of doing something. He wasn't as all-around dumb as he acted. He was smart enough, for sure, to pull the tired, helpless bit exactly when it suited him.

And just now it suited him. "My back," he moaned piteously, rubbing the small of his back. "I got to rest, Willis."

"Don't pull that baby shit on me," Willis said. "I'm not your Gramma, Richard." One afternoon Richard's grandmother had come looking for him. Maybe checking up to make sure Willis was doing what he was being paid to do. She was a nice-looking old lady, wearing a blue pants suit with jewel-rimmed glasses hanging on a chain around her neck. And she was nice to Willis, but what got him was the way she talked to Richard. "Honey," and "sweetheart," and "darling boy." She'd wiped his face, and cleaned his glasses, and held his hand like he was about four years old. Lucky for Richard she even let him go off to school, Willis had thought, watching them walk down the street together.

"My Gramma's nice, Willis. I love her."

"Yeah, but she spoils you, Richard. That's why you've got a fat ass."

Richard twisted around to see his behind. "I don't have a fat ass, either. Don't say those words. You say those words all the time. Miss Herman says people won't like you."

That was another thing that teed Willis off. Richard was always bringing up Miss Herman. Miss Herman says, Miss Herman does, Miss Herman this and Miss Herman that. Willis knew all he wanted to know about the suspicious Miss Herman. "Come on, get up," he said shortly, "we're going to try that standing broad jump again."

"Again?" Richard protested.

"Again," Willis said. He hadn't forgotten Mr. Hayfoot's saying another boy had tried to teach Richard and failed. Willis didn't want to fail. He hated losing. They went back along the creek to the regular place they worked out. Then, standing on the line and swinging his arms, Richard tripped over his shoelaces before he even jumped. It was the last straw for Willis in a long frustrating day.

"Tie your fuckin' laces," he yelled. Richard's laces were always flapping around loose.

Richard whirled the laces together, then knotted them.

"No," Willis said. "*Tie* them."

"Gramma ties my laces in the morning. She doesn't let me. She won't let me tie them, Willis. She'll be mad at me if I tie them."

"Don't give me that stuff. You're not fooling me, Richard! You don't know how to tie your laces, and you don't even try to learn. Now watch me." Willis knelt and tied his shoelaces. Richard watched, breathing heavily, but when he attacked his own laces again, he got the same messy tangle.

How could anyone be so stupid? Willis wondered furiously. Never before had he realized the hundreds and thousands of little things he knew, that he'd always known, that he couldn't even remember anyone teaching him. "You're stupid," he exclaimed. In the back of his mind he was remembering his own stupid mistake with Rabbit earlier in the day. "Just plain stupid."

The anxious smile faded from Richard's lips. "Why are you being mean to me?" He looked ready to cry.

Willis couldn't stand that big begging face. "Shut up! Shut up! You're a hopeless idiot."

Harry Mazer

Maddened with frustration, he whirled and ran off.

He ran across the footbridge, up a hill, then followed a curving road with overhanging trees. Around him were expensive houses. He ran on. He was through. Finished! Done! He quit! He couldn't teach Richard anything. It didn't matter how much money Mr. Hayfoot paid. Richard was hopeless! He ran harder, pushing himself over every hill. By the time he circled back to the creek he was calmer. He was surprised to find Richard still sitting in the path, exactly where he'd left him.

"What are you doing sitting on the ground?" Willis said. "Get up."

Richard shook his head. His legs were sprawled out, he was staring off into space.

"What's the matter with you?" Willis said.

"You said idiot to me."

"Oh, come on, nobody ever said idiot to you before?" Willis assumed a hearty tone. "I've been called idiot lots of times. Big deal. It doesn't bother me. Come on, get up." He shook Richard by the shoulder.

Richard swung his head back and forth negatively. "Going to sit here. Won't go anyplace."

"It's going to get dark pretty soon."

"Don't care. Going to sit here."

"You can't sit here all night!"

"Can too." Richard wiped his nose. "Sit here all night and sit here all day. Sit here forever and forever."

Willis sighed. "Listen, I didn't mean that about you being an idiot."

"You said it."

"It was just—nothing. Just a word. So what? Forget it."

Richard looked crookedly up at him. "I'm a retard."

Willis felt a jolt in his stomach. He had never expected to hear Richard say that. "No, you're not."

"Yes. I'm retarded. I know about it. It's not nice. It means stupid."

Willis didn't know what to say. *Yeah, kid, you're right. Retarded is stupid.* He felt impatient, and at the same time sort of sorry for Richard. It surprised him that Richard knew he was a retard. "How long you going to sit there?" he said, again trying for a cheerful hearty tone. "You don't see me sitting on the ground."

"Retards sit on the ground," Richard said miserably.

"Stop calling yourself a retard!"

"Retard, retard, retard!"

"Shut up," Willis said violently. He paced up and down. What was he getting so upset about? He must have called Richard a retard a million times, only not to his face. And he was a retard, that was the stone truth. And Richard knew it. It crossed Willis's mind that one way or the other, most people were usually lying to Richard. Either calling him an idiot, or trying to pretend nothing was wrong with him. Just like he was trying to pretend now.

"Retarded only means you're sort of slow," Willis said. "Like, it's harder for you to learn stuff than other people. So what? Some people learn stuff fast, and they're still stupid. Like Bucky Spivak and Rabbit Slavin."

"They're not retarded."

"They might as well be."

"What?" Richard said.

"Never mind." Willis knelt down and regarded Richard. "You can do things, plenty of things. Look at the new stuff you're learning. Sit-ups, and jumping jacks, and I bet you're going to get that standing broad jump pretty good, and—"

Richard sniffled up his snot. "But I can't tie my laces."

Willis sighed. "Well, let's try it again and see if you can this time." He knelt behind Richard, without much hope of success, took his hands, and guided them through the motions. "See? That's all there is to it."

"Do it again," Richard said. "Hold my hands."

Willis guided Richard's fingers again, and then several more times.

"Again," Richard said.

Willis shook his head. He'd had enough. It was making him nervous. "Do it yourself this time."

"You do it." Richard pointed to him.

"No. You." Willis narrowed his eyes. "Richard, *try*." That was the magic word with Richard.

He clamped his tongue between his teeth, threw the laces left and right, and ended with a loose, but perfect, tie. "I did it," he yelled in astonishment. "Willis, I tied my shoelaces!"

"And about time," Willis said. But it felt good to finally get Richard to do something he'd never been able to do before, even something as basic as tying a shoelace.

That evening, flushed with his success with Richard, he told his mother the story. "That's really nice," his mother said. "Maybe, Willis, you'll go to college and be a teacher." She had never said anything like that before. But with his father still off the stuff, she was feeling really good these days.

"Yeah, Mom, I can see it now. I'll teach shoelace tying." He made her laugh.

"Who's tying what?" his father said, coming into the kitchen. Five weeks on the wagon had changed his father. The nervousness and irritability had worn off. His father's face was relaxed, he'd put on some weight, he made jokes. Willis was keeping his fingers crossed. Whenever he thought about it he knocked on wood. He didn't want to believe yet. Five weeks was a long time, but not long enough.

"What's this about tying laces?" his father said again.

"It's this kid Richard, Pop. The one I'm teaching, remember?"

His father nodded. "Your mother told me something, but I forget the little details."

"I'm doing exercises and stuff with him. It's a regular job; his father is paying me three bucks an hour."

His father's eyebrows went up. "Three dollars an hour? Maybe I take that job myself. How old is this boy?"

"Sixteen," Willis said. He could almost frame his father's next words.

"Sixteen, and you have to teach him to tie his shoelaces!"

He should have known not much escaped his father. Not when he was sober. "Pop, this kid is a little slow, see—"

"Slow?"

"You know—he's in the special class."

"Ha! A dumbbell. We had the special class for dumbbells, too."

"He's not that dumb, Pop. You just got to tell him everything a couple times."

"Sure, sure," his father said. "Listen, my son, it's not good to be too much with the dumb ones."

"It's just a job, Pop."

His father nodded. "Okay, my son, you know what you're doing, ay?" He fingered his hair, then pulled his forelock down over his eyes. "Now tell me, since you're so smart, do I need a haircut?"

"No," Willis said, "your hair looks okay."

"Ha! You're wrong. I look like a bear. Louise, you want to give me a haircut?"

"Why not?" His mother got the scissors from the drawer. "Clear everything away, boys."

Willis cleared the table while his father spread newspapers under a chair and sat down. "To the collar in back, Louise, and cover the bare spot where the grass don't grow."

"Ray, you fool, your hair's thick as ever."

His father's fingers touched the top of his

head, then probed the deep vertical lines on his cheeks. "I'm getting old. These lines—"

"What lines?" Mrs. Pierce appealed to Willis. "Do you see any lines, Willis?"

Willis shook his head. "No lines, Pop." He liked the expression on his father's face. "Hey, Pop, remember the way you showed up Smitty? That fat foreman." Willis and his father laughed. "I know a bully just like him," Willis went on. "One of those guys who has to have his own way, or else." A shadow crossed Willis's mind. Rabbit threatening him. He pushed the thought away.

His father waved his hand disdainfully. "That Smitty. Alcohol's rotting his brains." Now that he was sober, Willis's father was down on all drinkers, even those who kept it to a glass or two after work. "What do they need it for? Fools. It's poison. Would any sane man swallow poison straight?"

His father's hair fell on the newspaper as his mother snipped away. "You know better than anyone," she said softly. She stepped back and examined her work. "Hey, I'm a terrific barber. Maybe I should change jobs."

"Wait till I see what you've done to me," his father said, winking at Willis. It was a good evening, one of the best Willis could ever remember with his parents.

CHAPTER 10

Willis jogged along the creek, Richard alongside him. It was a clear cool day, the best kind of day for jogging, and Willis would have liked to let go and run as fast as he could, but he restrained himself. Richard was doing okay keeping up with him, and only beginning to puff a little. Richard's wind had really improved. Willis was thinking about pointing this out to Mr. Hayfoot on Saturday when another jogger appeared ahead of him, running toward them.

The first thing Willis noticed was that the

guy was wearing yellow shorts over gray sweat pants. Someone from the school team. A message raced from his eyes to his brain and then to his feet, slowing them down, telling him that the news was bad. The runner was Kinsella.

Here he was, side by side with Richard, as if they were the best of friends, and there was one of Rabbit's trusty lieutenants running straight toward them. And it was too late to do anything about it. So Willis just kept moving, toward Kinsella and then past him, not looking at him or breaking his stride. All the time, talking to himself. Why should he care who saw him? He could run anywhere he wanted, and with anyone he chose. He didn't have to explain himself, and especially not to Kinsella.

But it wasn't Kinsella worrying him. It was Rabbit's knowing he was running with Richard. Kinsella would throw that tidbit of information to Rabbit, and it would be like giving a dog a bone. Willis could see Rabbit snapping it up. His stomach tightened. And just then he became aware that Richard was no longer running by his side.

He glanced back, then groaned. Kinsella was holding Richard by the arm. And Richard was blabbing. Willis could see the familiar eager smile on his face, see his mouth going, and his hands flying around as he talked.

"Richard," he yelled, starting back. "Come on, Richard." What he wanted to say was *Shut up, Richard!*

"And I do fifteen pull-ups," Richard was saying proudly as Willis approached. "I run one mile. Pretty soon I'll run two miles. Willis is teaching me everything. He's my coach, he's the fastest runner, he's—"

Willis yanked Richard away from Kinsella. The word "coach" rang mockingly in Willis's head.

Kinsella raised his long nose into the air, sniffing out the situation. "Hey, there, Pierce. Richard here says you're teaching him to be a big track star. He says his coach can beat me in a race, day or night."

"You can beat him, can't you, Willis?"

Willis shoved Richard ahead. "Come on, jog." They started off again. Willis was upset. Lousy luck. Lousy, lousy luck that he'd run in to Kinsella. *Rabbit doesn't forget.* And now another reminder to Rabbit that Willis was around, that Rabbit had unfinished business with him.

"That the fastest you can run?" Kinsella had come up behind him. He was so close the hair on Willis's nape bristled. "Run faster, little coach! I'm falling asleep."

Willis kept his pace steady. He didn't turn, speak, or acknowledge Kinsella's presence. Suddenly Kinsella's voice exploded in his ear. "Move! You're blocking my way." He lurched into Willis, knocking him off his feet, then raced past, kicking up his feet like a long yellow dog. He turned, smiling. "What's the matter, shorty? Can't stay on your feet? Maybe you been hitting the bottle too hard."

Willis's heart bounded fiercely inside his chest. His rush forward caught himself and then Kinsella by surprise.

But Kinsella was swift. He leaped aside, escaping Willis's hands, and then he was off. Willis ran after him. The race was on. They raced down the footpath paralleling the creek, veering in and out around a kid on a bike, a couple of girls, and a car parked on the grass. Kinsella was outdistancing him. He was getting away.

Willis ran hard. He had to catch Kinsella. Had to . . . had to . . . had to . . . The words pounded in his feet. It was Rabbit he was chasing. Rabbit . . . *Pull down his pants. . . . Rabbit doesn't forget. . . .* Images of Rabbit flashed through his mind. Rabbit banging his head against the wall. Rabbit giving him a raised fist. And Kinsella was there, grinning, mocking. . . .

As they approached the open fields, Willis

forced a burst of speed. Kinsella looked over his shoulder. Willis had closed the distance between them. Kinsella raced past a clump of willow trees, veered sharply around a play area, and ran straight up a hill. That was a mistake. Willis ate up hills. He could run as fast going uphill as most kids ran down.

He caught Kinsella just before the crest, raced past, then whirled around, fist raised, one hand on his heaving chest.

Kinsella couldn't catch his breath. "You— better—stay—away—from—me," he gasped. He was scared. Afraid Willis was going to hit him.

Willis stood over him. How many times had he imagined himself racing against Kinsella, and winning? Kinsella, the fastest feet on the track team. Kinsella, the big jock hero. Kinsella, Rabbit's chief man. And now he'd done it. He'd beaten Kinsella in a race, beaten him fair and square. He almost laughed out loud. Hit Kinsella? It was the farthest thing from his mind. What he had done was a thousand times better than a million blows. Better than anything he could think of. No, there was one thing that could have made it better. If Rabbit had seen him do it, that would have made this moment perfect.

CHAPTER 11

It was getting dark as Willis left Richard at his corner and headed for home, running easily. Once again he went over in his mind his race with Kinsella the day before, savoring the memory of every detail. If there were just some way of telling Marion Bouchard how he'd beaten the big K. Last night he'd actually dreamed he was telling her. The dream had been so real. He had seen the beaded fringe on Marion's white jacket, and the links in the gold chain she wore around her neck. Then, when he woke up, he had felt a horrible sense of disappointment that there was no way he could think of to let her know.

Marion didn't even look at him anymore. More than ever she seemed to him like a queen sweeping through the halls of school. And if she was a queen, then he was just a lowly galley slave.

What if he stopped Sue Tyson sometime when she was alone and let her know about his race with Kinsella? Much as he disliked her, he could at least imagine himself talking to her. First he'd set her up, ask her who she thought was the fastest runner in school. Then she'd say Kinsella. And he'd tell her how he'd overtaken Kinsella, and drop a casual hint that she should let Marion know.

As he ran through the darkening streets, Willis glanced at the houses. Lights were coming on inside, and sometimes he could see people in the windows. Marion lived in one of these houses. Sue Tyson not far away. Could he really get up the nerve to tell Sue? And even if he did, what made him think she'd oblige him by telling Marion. *If* she even believed him.

Rounding the corner of Villa, he looked up to his windows. Nobody home yet. His mother was working late tonight. And his father? A wave of heat went through Willis. It was Friday night, his father should have been home by now. Unless he was sitting in Pete's Bar. Willis's legs suddenly felt limp, and he stopped. He didn't feel like going up to the dark house. He turned aimlessly, and at that moment he was grabbed. Rabbit, Bucky, the rest of them. They'd been waiting for him in the shadows.

"Here he is, here's the teacher," Bucky said.

So Kinsella had told, Willis thought. And then Rabbit was jabbing his fingers into Willis's ribs. "You didn't ask my permission"— Jab!—"to be a teacher, Pierce." Jab! "Don't you know anything?" Jab! "Don't you know you got to ask Rabbit's permission?"

Willis was scared, but he tightened his lips, and concentrated on how he hated and despised Rabbit. Rabbit had to have his pack of followers. And he had to have somebody to kick around.

"Hey, you, answer me." Jab!

His ribs were already hurting. He made a noise under his breath.

"He's mocking you out, Rab," Sam cried, dancing around Willis with his fists raised. "He's mocking you out."

"Bash him, Rabbit, whyn't you bash him," the redheaded Dodge twins said excitedly. Grinning, they shoved up against Willis from both sides.

"Remember last time he got away from us," Bucky said. Only Kinsella wasn't present. He'd done his dirty work, giving Rabbit a reason for wiping out Willis.

They crowded him back, jamming him against a car. Someone kneed him in the groin. Willis cried out and bent over.

"He's talking now!"

Rabbit jabbed Willis again, another hard stiff jab in the ribs. "Say, 'I—will—not—teach—the —retard.'"

"Rab's talking to you, queer, Frenchie queer!"

"Open your mouth, you skinny Frog," Bucky said.

They were all pressing hard against him, getting themselves excited, like a pack of dogs on an animal they'd chased down. Willis could feel a beating coming. He looked for a way out. If he could break through, he could outrun them. Get out now, or forget it, he told himself. He took a breath, put his head down and plunged between the Dodge twins. He took them by surprise and made it. But in a moment they were after him.

He wanted to get to the safety of his home, but he was going the wrong way. He raced around the block, then cut back down a long narrow alley between his building and the next one. In back of the building where the janitor stacked the garbage cans was a small walled-in yard. A dead end, except for a door leading to the cellar of his building. Once inside, he'd be okay.

He was all the way to the back when he heard a shout. They'd found the alleyway, spotted him. He ran for the door, confidently pushed it. It didn't open. He pushed again. It didn't give. He threw his shoulder against it. Hit it again. It had to open.

He heard them pounding down the alley. He looked around, then leaped for the fire escape above him. He caught the bottom rung of the ladder, but they were there now. They grabbed him around the legs and dragged him to the ground.

Panicked, he punched out wildly, hit somebody's face.

"Bastard!"

His head cracked against the brick wall. Dazed, he crumpled to the ground. He tried to get to his feet. They grunted as they punched him. He tasted blood in his mouth, then he must have blacked out.

A bell rang in his ear. Time to get up. Turn off the alarm. The bell was ringing. Get up. His father hated to be late to work. Didn't they hear the stupid bell ringing?

He was flat on the ground. There was a wet place under his cheek.

"You hit him too hard."

Someone prodded him with a foot. "He's faking it."

"You practically killed him."

"What do you mean, *I* killed him. You hit him, too."

"Let's go!"

The scrape of footsteps. Then silence. Willis kept his eyes closed. He wasn't going to move. It was cool beneath his cheek. Tar smell. Good. A breeze blew through the alley. He heard the chink of dishes somewhere. Then a radio.

After a while he got to his feet. He found a piece of newspaper and wiped his nose gingerly. A gob of blood came out. One eye was throbbing. He moved cautiously back up the alley. The light from the street hurt his eyes. His own hunched-over image in a car window startled him.

He went upstairs. The apartment was dark. He put ice in a towel and stood in front of the bathroom sink, eyes closed, icing his swollen eye. He was glad when he heard his father come in, but he locked the bathroom door.

"Is that you, Willis?" His father rapped on

the door. "I stopped and got fried fish and chips."

"Not hungry." He went to his room and lay down with the iced cloth against his eye. He slept. It was dark when he woke. There was a blanket over him. He drifted off. They were pounding him. Forcing him to eat dog turds. He bolted up in the dark room, gagging.

He slept again. Then his father was in the room. The light came on. "Shut the light!" he said. He felt awful.

"What's the matter, Willis? Don't you want some food?" His father bent over him. "What happen to your face?"

"Shut the light!" He threw himself around, facing the wall.

His father turned off the light and sat on the edge of the bed. He patted Willis's shoulder. "You had some trouble, ay? They hurt you bad."

His sympathy made Willis's eyes dampen and his chest suddenly swell to splitting. He wanted to say something to his father, but not about the beating. He didn't want his father to feel ashamed of him. "Pop," he said hoarsely, "I ever tell you about this guy in school who can run faster than anybody?"

"He flies, ay?" his father said.

Willis nodded. "But I fly faster. I beat him running the other day."

126

"When I was a boy in Quebec," his father said, "I was a good runner, too. Nobody catches me. They run fast, I run faster. And all summer, I run barefoot. No socks, no sneakers, just bare naked feet."

"Sounds nice, Pop," Willis said. His eye was throbbing. But he was glad they weren't talking about the beating. The heat of his father's hand on his shoulder soaked through the aches and soreness in his body. "Don't go away, Pop," he said. His father was still sitting there when he fell asleep.

CHAPTER 12

"Hello, Willis." Miss Herman stopped Willis on the stairs. He was on his way up from shop. "How's everything?"

"All right," he said warily.

"That was clever the way you taught Richard the difference between left and right," she said. "He's really got it down now." Willis had stuck a piece of green tape on Richard's right foot and taught him, "Right foot, green foot, left foot, plain foot."

"It was nothing," Willis said. She had some scent on her that was making him dizzy.

"Don't say that," she said. "It was very definitely something. What you're doing, Willis, working with Richard, is so fine."

Willis reddened. "I'm being paid." She must have heard that best-friend junk from Richard. She was standing on the stairs above him, so he didn't know where to look. His eyes were on a level with her waist. Up or down, either way he felt embarrassed.

She gave him a smile. "Paid? So am I being paid. But that's not the only reason I'm doing my work." She tapped him lightly on the head with a folder and went past him and down the stairs.

Willis looked after her for a moment, then went on, a little stunned by the encounter. She had acted as if she liked him. As if she thought he was someone special, or something.

So many things were changing. Not working out with Richard, he didn't mean that. Right after the beating, he had felt like washing his hands of Richard once and for all. A million dollars couldn't make up for having his head taken off. But the idea of giving up had made him furious. So he'd just gone on with the training as if nothing had happened. He'd had a black eye, a swollen mouth and nose. Plenty of wise questions. "Who'd you run into, King

Kong?" "Yeah, with his brother." He'd brushed off kids' questions like that, met Richard by the footbridge every day, and in school and on the streets walked warily.

Then one afternoon he ran straight into Rabbit coming out of Coach Weber's office. It was strange, all right. Their eyes met. Rabbit bared his teeth. But Willis passed him with only the smallest tremor. He thought, *Well, what else can he do to me?* And the minute he thought it, it was as if he could straighten up again.

Every day, almost every minute, since that first time when Rabbit had grabbed him on Fitch Road, Willis had been waiting for the beating. And in a way the waiting had been worse than the beating itself. It had gone on and on and on. But now he wasn't waiting anymore. It would never be that bad again, and so he just wasn't afraid in the same way. With that recognition, he started feeling lucky.

That was something new, all right. A kind of light feeling he'd never noticed before. As if someone had pulled this enormous stone off his chest. It had to do with his father, too. A lot to do with his father. He'd been sober for going on eight weeks now, and feeling stronger every day. And the stronger his father felt, the stronger and luckier Willis felt. His luck had been bad for so long, and now it was going the other way.

Everything was going good. Mornings he woke up thinking about the day ahead. About running, teaching Richard, school. He got a 90 on a shop drawing. An 85 on a history quiz. A lot different from the 20s and 30s he used to pull. He showed his mother every passing paper.

"Very good, my boy," she said.

"Just luck," he said, and behind his back he crossed his fingers.

That afternoon he went into the variety store near the shopping plaza with Richard to help him buy notebook paper. He steered Richard to the stationery counter and handed a pack of lined paper to the girl behind the counter. "Richard, give her your money."

"It's in my secret pocket, Willis. Turn your head and close your eyes. Don't look."

Willis leaned against the counter, watching the girl from the corner of his eye.

Richard put his money into the girl's hand. "You're tall like me," he said. "And you got pretty rings on your fingers, and pretty bracelets on your wrist." He gave the salesgirl a big winning smile.

Her bracelets jangled as she slipped the paper into a bag. "Here you are, good-looking."

Richard touched the chain around the girl's neck. "Let me see what's on this pretty necklace." His big hand was right on her skin. Did Richard know what he was doing? Willis's whole body was hot, like it was his own hand. He looked at the girl's breasts. The Big Looker, that was him. If he could do it with his eyes, he'd be the champion of champions.

The girl had a ring at the end of the chain. "What is that," Richard said, "your religion?"

"It's my boyfriend's ring."

"If he doesn't know you've got it, I won't tell."

The girl laughed. "Funny!"

Richard laughed, too, a loud bellow. "If he doesn't know you've got it, I won't tell," he repeated. He looked expectantly at the girl. "You're supposed to say, Funny!"

"Funny, funny, funny." The girl raised her eyebrows at Willis, then turned to another customer.

"Come on, Richard." Willis led the way out of the store. "Do you have to act so dumb?" he said outside. He wanted to tell Richard, *Keep your mouth shut. Don't smile so much. Try to act normal.*

Wounded, Richard stared at him. "I didn't do anything bad."

"You were pawing that girl all over," Willis said. "That's not the way to act."

"I like girls, Willis."

"So do I. So what? You don't see me putting my hands all over them."

"I like pretty girls, Willis. I like to touch them. Isn't that all right? It's nice, Willis. That girl was nice, she thought I was funny. Do you think she'd be my girlfriend?"

"No. Now, that's a dumb question and you know it."

"No, I don't. Why is it a dumb question?"

"She's got a boyfriend. Besides, what do you need a girlfriend for?"

"I told you, I like girls," Richard shouted, getting excited. "I want to kiss them. I want to kiss pretty girls. Do you know Marion Bouchard? She likes me, Willis. Do you know what? One time Marion kissed me."

It was really stupid, but Willis felt the sting of jealousy. Richard was tall and not so bad-looking. And Marion was nice to him. Willis had never forgotten the time he'd seen her combing Richard's hair. She would never do anything like that for him.

"Come on," he said crossly, "let's get over to the creek."

He glanced sideways at the big boy. Physically he was as developed as any 16-year-old. Did that mean he thought about girls the way other boys did, the way Willis did? But Richard was such a baby! You could make him laugh or cry practically with a glance. What girl would really want Richard for a boyfriend? She'd have to be retarded like him. Willis remembered a pretty, slender girl he'd seen coming out of Miss Herman's room one day. She'd had dark hair tied back with a red ribbon. She wore blue jeans and a gray zip-down sweat shirt. He liked the way she looked, but he could tell she was retarded. Why didn't Richard go with that girl?

"Richard, aren't there any girls in your class you like?"

"No. I like Marion."

"How about Sue Tyson?" Willis said.

"Marion's prettier," Richard said, and seeing that he'd made Willis laugh, he said it again.

Saturday, as usual, Mr. Hayfoot came to watch them work out for a while, before paying Willis for the preceding week. He came strolling up, hands in the pockets of his jacket. Richard had just completed his warm-up, and Willis was fooling around with him, doing a little arm wrestling.

"We're taking a break," he said, looking up at Mr. Hayfoot. But then he had Richard go through his paces again for his father's benefit.

"Watch me, Poppy. Watch me do my push-ups," Richard said. "Look at my muscles. I'm getting such big muscles, like Willis's," he boasted.

It was true—Richard was doing everything better. Running up to two miles a day, and broad jumping a little over five feet. Every day he did a little better than the day before.

Leaning against a tree, Mr. Hayfoot had a pleased expression. "How do you think he'll do in Field Day, Willis?"

"I don't know, Mr. Hayfoot. It depends on the competition. I guess it'll be pretty fierce."

"As long as he doesn't have to compete against you, Willis." Mr. Hayfoot laughed, smoothing his mustache. "You're not entering the standing broad jump, are you?"

Willis shook his head. "I'm not going into Field Day."

"You're not!" Mr. Hayfoot really looked surprised. "Why not?"

"I don't go in for that stuff, Mr. Hayfoot."

"What stuff is that?"

Willis raised his shoulders. "Well, team stuff and Field Days. Showing off. I mean it's okay for Richard and all, but I run for myself. I run all the time, but I do it for myself. If I was going to enter, anyway, it would be running, because that's what I do." Then he was embarrassed that he'd said so much.

Shaking his head, Mr. Hayfoot blew out his lips in a gesture of surprise. "I think you're making a big mistake, Willis. A boy like you— you should be on the team. You should be in that Field Day."

Willis shrugged. Mr. Hayfoot saw him as this extremely fortunate kid with not a worry in the world, but there were things he didn't know.

"You're a natural athlete," Mr. Hayfoot went on. "You're a little small, but you compensate with speed and agility. I've watched you now for five, six weeks, and I know what I'm talking about. Not to put too fine a point on it, I was an athlete myself, and I know what I'm talking about. Let me ask you something, Willis. What about college? Ever think of a sports scholarship?"

"College? Me?" Was Mr. Hayfoot kidding? He'd never seriously thought of it. Sure, he and his mother had joked about it that once, but that was just kidding around. What he might do when he got out of school was go into the Navy. He thought he'd like that. He knew he didn't want to work in a factory. Being closed in like that all the time—no, he wouldn't like that.

"There are scholarships around for boys like you who are outstanding athletes," Mr. Hayfoot said. "Well, in your case, I'd have to say a potential outstanding athlete. You'd have to prove yourself. Start participating on the teams, show what you can do. Nobody gives away scholarships for nothing. It's performance that counts."

Mr. Hayfoot put a big hand on Willis's shoulder. "Don't throw away your potential. Don't throw away the wonderful things God has given you." Mr. Hayfoot's face flushed with emotion. "Willis, you've helped Richard a lot. I appreciate everything. I hope you think about what I've said, and anytime you want to talk to me, you feel free."

Once again that light lucky feeling came over Willis. No grown-up, no one outside his family, had ever thought about him before. Now there was Mr. Hayfoot, Miss Herman, and for that matter Coach Weber. He had stopped Willis specially in the corridor only the other day and told him the Field Day lists were still open and he hoped Willis would sign up.

After Mr. Hayfoot left, Willis ran sprints with Richard, then let him take a rest. Willis looked up at the trees brushing back and forth against the sky. The green leaves and the blue sky. He'd never seen anything so beautiful. He thought of Marion. Willis and Marion. Marion and Willis. *Hi, Marion.* That's what he'd say next time he saw her. Just pick up his hand, wave, and say it. *Hi, Marion!*

Hi, Willis. You sign up for Field Day yet?

Sure did, Marion.

Great! You've got so much talent. You've got natural athletic ability. You shouldn't hide it.

"Whew, whew, I'm bushed," Richard said, falling back on the grass. "Whew, I'm panting, Willis."

"You don't hear me panting," Willis said, sitting down.

"You got good wind, Willis. Good wind," Richard said respectfully.

"I might enter Field Day," Willis said, testing the idea aloud. In a way he'd been thinking about it ever since the first posters went up, but not seriously. Just imagining stuff like beating Kinsella. But now, saying it, the possibility began to seem real. All he had to do was tell

Coach Weber. He shifted uneasily. All his life he'd avoided pushing himself in front of other people's faces. And here he was thinking about Field Day, where hundreds of people would be watching.

He saw himself on the starting line, crouched low, then racing out in front of the other runners. His father would be in the stands cheering him on, wearing a snappy-looking shirt, maybe a tie, his shoes brushed up to a terrific gloss. He'd see Willis flashing around the track, past Kinsella, past everyone, breaking through the white tape at the finish line. *And the winner of the 220 is . . . Willis Pierce!*

The fresh heat of the May sun baked through Willis. "I can beat Kinsella," he said. "I did it once. I can do it again. I can beat any of them."

"Yes, you can, Willis, yes you can."

Willis raised his head. Richard had his sneakers off and was sitting up picking his toes. "Yes, you can, Willis, yes you can."

There was one person who would be ready to chew nails if he beat Kinsella. Rabbit Slavin. To see Rabbit's eyes drop out would be worth anything.

"And you know who else is going to be impressed?" he said. "There's a girl in school, she's going to see something she never saw before when Willis the flying Frenchman comes flying around that track."

"Zoom, zoom, zoom!" Richard said.

"Don't you say a word about me entering Field Day," Willis said, twisting around and pinning Richard to the ground. He could smell the sun on Richard's skin. "This is a secret, Richard, so don't start your mouth going. No advertising. Anyway, I'm not even sure yet I'm going to do it."

But that night he mentioned Field Day to his father. He did it right after supper, when his father settled back for his cigarette and coffee. "Pop, I think I'm going to sign up. Will you come and watch me?"

"When is it?" his father said.

"Next Saturday."

"Saturday, ay? Well, I might have something important to do on Saturday."

"Pop, you don't have anything to do on Saturday!"

"What, what, look at that face!" His father laughed. "Okay, can't you take no teasing? I'll come. Sure, you sign up. But better not fall on your face. I'm coming to see you win the big race."

Monday morning first thing, Willis went to Coach Weber's office. The coach, wearing a short-sleeved white shirt, showing thick hairy arms, was sitting behind his desk working on some papers.

"Coach," Willis said, as he stepped into the office, "I want to—" He stopped. They weren't alone, as he'd thought. Rabbit was sprawled deep in a chair with a magazine. Involuntarily, Willis stepped back.

"What can I do for you, Pierce?" Mr. Weber said.

"I want to sign up for Field Day."

Rabbit sat up, rolling the magazine into his fist. "Coach! You can't let him sign up."

"It's not too late," Mr. Weber said. "The lists are still open. Glad you decided, Willis."

Rabbit batted the rolled-up magazine against his open palm. The look he gave Willis was pure poison. Willis stared blankly back. Being so close to Rabbit still made him feel a little sick to his stomach.

Mr. Weber took some papers from his desk. "You'll be doing track events, won't you?" Willis nodded. "Two-twenty, and the half?" Willis nodded again. "Both. Good." Mr. Weber made a notation on the sheet. "Okay. You're all set."

Willis felt curiously light-headed. It was done now.

"Well," Mr. Weber said, "I hope this means

141

you'll come out for track next year, Pierce." He put the Field Day list back in his drawer. "Good luck. See you Saturday. Think you'll win them both?" he added cheerfully as Willis opened the door.

"Coach," Rabbit grated, getting up, "Big K will run his ass into the ground!"

At that Willis couldn't control his face. Whatever Kinsella had told Rabbit, he sure hadn't told him how Willis had outrun him.

Rabbit followed him to the door. "What are you grinning about?" He jabbed savagely at Willis.

Willis jumped back, giving Rabbit the finger. "Wait and see!"

The next morning he left the apartment even before his parents were awake. It was dim and raining lightly as he ran through the streets. From now till Field Day he was going to run five miles every morning. He wanted to be in top condition.

As he ran, skirting the garbage cans left on the curb for collection, Willis felt everything in his life unscrambling, dropping into place. He was going to run in Field Day. For the first time he was going to do something in public, and he was hardly even nervous about it. Well, Pierces could do things. They could run. They had nothing to hide. They were as good as anybody else.

He thought about the crowds that would turn out for Field Day. All the kids, the teachers, Miss Herman, parents, Mr. Hayfoot. His father, especially his father. He was going to win those races. His father was going to see him win. "That's my son!" His father would be so proud he'd never even think about drinking again.

Willis ran lightly and easily through the still-quiet streets. He felt as if he could run on and on, run forever with the same ease and lightness. Was he happy? He'd never put such a word to anything he felt, but that's what it must be. He was happy.

CHAPTER 13

Field Day. As Willis entered the field, the flag next to the school flapped against the metal pole. Crowds milled onto the field and across the oval track. Mr. Firstman, the vice-principal, speaking through a gray bullhorn, was asking people to stay off the track.

Willis straightened the legs on his sweat pants and scuffed his new track shoes in the dust. Kids barreled past him around the track. A hot-dog trailer stood on the green. Whole families streamed past the judges' table and climbed up into the wooden stands.

The standing broad jump was announced. Richard's event. Willis cut across the green. Buddy Ley greeted him. They slapped hands. "What are you doing here, Pierce?"

"Same thing you are, Ley." Buddy had on track clothes, too. It looked like everyone in school was going to participate in the field events. And here he was, doing what everyone else did. It was strange, but he liked the feeling it gave him. He felt more like everyone else, less of an outsider.

Then he came face to face with Sue Tyson and Marion. Sue in green gym shorts and green-and-yellow socks, and a matching green headband. She was going to run in the girls' track events. He stopped, nodded, smiled hopefully. Marion was in white, straight and tall and perfect, all in white. Her eyes skimmed the top of his head. He walked by. Had she smiled at him? Sue had, sort of, but not Marion.

A crowd had gathered to watch the broad jumpers. Richard was right in the middle, standing next to the coach. "When's my turn, Mr. Weber? Mr. Weber, Mr. Weber. Mr. Weber, when's my turn?"

The coach consulted his clipboard. "Pretty soon, Richard."

Mr. Hayfoot was chatting with Miss Herman.

He noticed Willis and called him over. He gave Willis a big smile. "Glad to see you here, Willis." And Miss Herman squeezed his hand. Out of school, with a Polaroid camera slung around her neck, she looked outdoorsy and fresh. "Good luck on your race, Willis," she said. "I know you're going to do well." He smiled and shrugged. The back of his neck was hot.

Finally Richard's name was called. There was a cheer from the kids in his class. Richard rushed to the starting line, hands above his head, and danced around.

"Stand back behind the white line," Mr. Weber said. "No horseplay now."

"Show us what you can do, Richard," Miss Herman called. She snapped a picture of him.

"Jump to the moon," a kid from his class called. "Richard's going to jump to the moon."

Willis watched Richard expectantly. This past week he had broad-jumped six feet every single time. But Richard's first jump was a disaster. He sprang wildly, arms and legs flailing, then fell flat on his back, as if he'd forgotten everything Willis had taught him.

He scrambled to his feet, looking at Willis. "I stink, that was *awful*." He hit his fist into his hand.

On his second jump Richard was so cautious

he barely cleared four feet. Willis felt ashamed for Richard, ashamed for himself, too. He glanced at Mr. Hayfoot. All those weeks he'd spent with Richard, pushing him, training him, trying to get him to do things right—what for? So he could bomb in front of the whole school? He stepped forward and slapped Richard smartly on the butt. "Richard. Concentrate! You can do better than that."

Richard gave him a tense look. He scowled and shook his head. He was all knotted up. He'd never do a decent jump feeling like that. "Hey—" Willis shook Richard's arm, reminding himself that pushing Richard was always a big mistake. "Hey, Richie, loosen up. Take a deep breath. Come on, take another one. Remember how good you jumped yesterday? You can do it again."

Richard sighed deeply. He bent his knees, then stood up and took another deep breath and started again. Bent his knees, swung his arms, and sprang forward. Good motion, good lift, good distance. He landed cleanly. Mr. Weber read the tape. "Six feet, ten and one half inches," he announced.

Willis was stunned. He threw an arm around Richard's neck. "You did it, boy. You did it!" It was the best jump Richard had ever made. A fantastic jump. The kids from Richard's class crowded around him.

"You big jumper," said the cute dark-haired girl Willis remembered. "You big pretty jumper."

Mr. Hayfoot caught Willis's arm. His face was one big smile. "Terrific, wasn't that terrific, Willis?"

"He really did good, Mr. Hayfoot. I'm glad."

Mr. Hayfoot shook Willis's hand again and again. "Well, you've got to take the credit, Willis. You just have to take the credit."

Finally, Willis moved off, looking around for his father. He couldn't understand why his father hadn't showed up yet. Too bad he missed seeing Richard jump. Well, he'd tell his father about it later, and repeat what Mr. Hayfoot had said to him.

The 220 was announced over the bullhorn. Willis jogged to the starting line, stretched and bent, loosening up. He was starting to feel nervous, aware of all the people, all those eyes. Kinsella, Williams, all the best runners were in this race. He told himself relax, relax, take a deep breath, the same advice he'd given Richard. But he was upset because his father wasn't there. He kept looking around for him.

The starting blocks were new to Willis. He

glanced at the runners on either side and copied them, squatting down, one foot forward, one back, rising on his hands. The signal was given. The gun went off. Willis came up looking at the backs of the other runners. The last one to get off.

A roar went up as they started. Willis drove forward, pumping his legs and arms, running catch-up all the way. It seemed he hardly had time to get his speed up and the race was over. Jim Williams, a tall wiry black kid wearing the track-team jersey, came in first. Kinsella placed second, and Willis didn't place at all.

He stepped off into the center grass gasping for breath. Disappointed in himself. He saw Rabbit, Bucky, and Sam on the side, looking at him and laughing. Hands on his hips he circled the field slowly, scanning the crowd. Telling himself not to get discouraged. The 220 really wasn't his event. He wasn't a sprinter, he needed time to get up his speed. He went full around the field and still didn't see his father. He had come in late the night before and was dead asleep when Willis got up this morning.

Willis brushed his hair uneasily. A picture of Pete's Bar flashed into his mind. He kept moving. No, not after all this time. No, he wouldn't. Not now. No, please.

Harry Mazer

When the half mile was called, he trotted to the starting line. Kinsella, long and sleek, was next to him. Willis didn't look up. He didn't look at anyone. He tried to clear his mind. *Concentrate. Run your own race.* But anxiety about his father nibbled at the edges of his mind. He took several deep breaths, filling his lungs with good clean air. He thought of the times he'd run through the streets or along the creek.

He had the sudden intuition that his father was out in the stands now, watching him. He glanced around, and the gun went off, catching him by surprise. Again he started a moment behind the other runners. It was like the first race, but this time he moved up on the first turn to where the runners were packed together. Kinsella was already far in the lead, his back straight, moving so smoothly he seemed motionless, only his long pale hair lifted by the wind.

Willis kept his eyes on Kinsella, establishing a strong steady pace, not letting the taller boy increase the distance between them. At the halfway mark, when they'd gone around the track once, he began closing the gap. Now that he was in motion, everything was okay. His doubts had vanished. This was what he knew. This was what he could do.

"Shorty, Shorty." A chant rose from the stands. "Go, Shorty, go." Willis realized the crowd was cheering him. "Go, go, go, go . . ." Energy shot hotly through his body. He drove forward through the curve, ignoring the tearing in his throat, his pounding heart, listening only to the rhythm of his feet repeating *Catch Kinsella . . . Catch Kinsella . . . Catch Kinsella . . .*

Rabbit ran along the edge of the track shouting to Kinsella to *go*. Kinsella looked back, then increased his pace. Willis lengthened his stride. They were locked together now, just the two of them, leaving the other runners behind. They approached the final turn. Willis was flying now, his body free, his feet barely touching ground. The gap between himself and Kinsella closed. The crowd roared. He thought Kinsella was holding something back for a last kick, but Willis couldn't hold anything back. He had to go. He approached Kinsella as effortlessly as if he were skimming over water.

He passed Kinsella. A cheer rose from the stands. Alone now. Nobody in front of him. His heart pounded in his throat. He lifted his legs higher, drove forward with every ounce of strength. He was going to win. Then as he came out of the turn he saw his father at last. He was at the edge of the track by the stands, struggling in the grip of two men. His father's jacket was open, he was trying to break free. He was yelling.

Willis's feet turned to lead. His father wrenched free of the two men and rushed toward him. Kinsella passed Willis, and moments later another runner. Willis crossed the finish line. He turned. His father was standing in the middle of the track, hands raised above his head, cheering. Willis put down his head and ran toward him. "Get off the track," he said. "Please! The race is over."

His father threw his arms around Willis. "You won, my son, ay? Ay? Ay?" His father clung to him in drunken warmth. His father's embrace . . . the gagging smell of booze. Willis felt nauseous. He felt every eye on them.

"Kinsella . . . Jones . . . Pierce . . ." The names were boomed out over the bullhorn. He'd come in third.

His father leaned heavily on him. He stank, that sweet boozy sickening smell. "I'll take you home," Willis said. "You want to go home, don't you?" He half supported, half dragged his father off the field and out through the gate onto the street.

CHAPTER 14

"You think I don't keep my promises, ay?" his father said. "I come to see you run, like I said. Come to see my son run. That's good. Don't tell me that's not good." His father's arm lay like an iron pipe across Willis's shoulders.

Willis walked doggedly, head down, saying nothing. His mind felt fogged with despair. He wanted to get off the street. There was too much light. He couldn't forget the eyes, all those eyes watching them.

In their building, in the darkness, his father

breathed heavily as they went up the stairs. Once, he stumbled and Willis caught him. Willis unlocked the door to their apartment. He went straight to his room and tore off his track clothes. He put on jeans and a T-shirt.

In the kitchen he drank a quart of milk standing by the refrigerator. The cold white liquid numbed his throat.

His father came out of the bathroom. "Make me a sandwich," he ordered. "I'm hungry." His accent was thick. It always came back when he drank.

Willis's hands trembled as he shoved together cheese and bread. It was all coming back to him in waves of heat and nausea. Leaning around the turn, passing Kinsella, the sound rising from the stands . . . *Go Shorty!* . . . And then his father appearing.

He pushed the sandwich across the table. His father poked at it, then pushed it back. "Mustard on cheese. How many times I have to tell you? You're so stupid sometimes." His mood had changed, turned aggressive. "Mustard on cheese, like bread on butter!"

Willis went to the cupboard. The mustard jar clattered to the table. He grabbed a knife, smeared the mustard thickly on the bread. He hated his father.

"Hey!" His father took a bite of the sandwich. "What's the matter with you? You ain't talked since I saw you. You ashamed because I don't talk good English in front of your smart friends?"

Sourness rose in Willis's throat.

"What's the matter?" his father demanded. "What are you looking at me for? You told me to come see you, run, ay. I come, ay."

"Yeah, you came," Willis burst out.

"So, why don't you smile? You don't have nothing to say to your father?"

"You came to Field Day drunk," Willis said hoarsely. "Don't you know what you did? Don't you know anything? You're still drunk!"

His father's lips twitched. He wiped his face. "So a man takes a couple of drinks. What's wrong with that? You and your mother—ha. A couple of stuck-up noses."

Willis stared at his father. His hatred choked him. Oh, God, he hated him. In a rush all his plans and thoughts and dreams flooded his mind. He'd believed his father, believed he was really on the wagon. He'd *believed.*

When he thought of the things he'd been thinking—college, scholarships, joining the team. It was all so fucking stupid. So pointless. He felt numb and listless. He just didn't want to sit here and look at his father's stupid twitching face. He started for the door.

"Hey, boy!" His father ordered him back. Willis stopped. He didn't want to obey, but he responded. Like a dog, he thought bitterly, despising himself.

"Sit down! You keep running all the time, you make me dizzy."

Willis leaned against the wall, eyes averted, arms crossed over the knot in his stomach. His father was looking at him and looking at him. A mean narrow-eyed look. Willis slid his back along the wall. He'd brought his father home, he'd fed him, what else did he want?

"Sit!" his father said. He caught Willis by the arm, yanked him around, forced him into a chair. "I told you. *Sit.*"

Willis slowly rubbed his arms. His father stood over him. "I'm the boss here." His feet were spread. "Am I the boss, or no?"

Willis hunched forward and stared hard at the floor. The drunken bastard. He was in a crazy mood.

"Hey, you. Answer me." Willis stubbornly kept his mouth shut. His father shook him to his feet. "Answer me! Answer me!" He slapped Willis around the head.

"*Boss,*" Willis said, spitting it out, his heart

filled with loathing. "Yes, boss, yes, you're the *boss* of the house."

His father punched him in the face. Willis tried to get away. His father pushed him back. He unbuckled his belt, and yanked it off. "Now I'll show you." The strap came down across Willis's shoulder. His eyes blurred. The belt came down again on his raised arm.

"You drunken son of a bitch, I wish you were dead," Willis screamed.

His father came at him again. He pushed his father away, then grabbed for the strap and wrestled it out of his father's hands. "Hey," his father exclaimed. "What are you doing?"

Willis threw the strap down. He didn't want to hit his father. But his father came at him again, crowding him against the wall. Willis hit out. He punched his father in the chest. He punched his father again and again, with both hands, fighting for his life. His heart was pounding with terror and rage.

He ran from the apartment. He fled down Villa Street. The world screamed at him. Car horns, sirens, screeching trucks. It was a world at war. He ran in a daze. Had he really hit his father? Had he dared do that? Never before. He saw his fist raised, saw the startled look on his father's face. He felt the impact of bone against bone. He heard his voice screaming. *I wish you were dead.*

Then another voice. *You don't hit your father, no matter what. You respect your father.* How many times had his mother said that to him? Over and over. Pounded it into his head. It was the Law. He kept running. There was nothing else to do.

CHAPTER 15

Willis stopped running somewhere along the creek. His legs were wobbly, his whole body felt heavy. He leaned against a tree. What now? He knew he didn't want to go home. Not now. Maybe never. He had taken too much from his father for too long. And now he'd hit him. He'd broken the Law. He'd go away. He didn't know where, but that didn't matter. Just away.

He followed the creek till he came to the railroad yards. It had started to drizzle. The pavement glistened. Cars had on their lights. He walked past the tracks, past small businesses, parking lots, a fenced-off lumberyard, then, in the midst of all the buildings, a small graveyard.

He lifted his thumb as a truck boomed past. It didn't matter where the driver was going. He just wanted a ride anywhere. Albany, Boston, New York. He was strong, he'd help the driver unload, earn his ride. He could sleep anywhere in good weather. If it rained he'd climb into the back of the truck. He'd keep going, keep getting rides, on and on, till he got to the end of the country, Canada, or the ocean.

He'd return to see his mother someday, but never his father. He raised his thumb again. The truck's lights bounced in the rain. No one stopped. He walked on, faster. The rain was falling hard. He pulled up his collar.

In a block of stores he stepped into a launderette to dry off. It was warm inside. Machines hummed. A girl in jeans with a red kerchief around her hair folded clothes in one corner. Willis bought peanut-butter crackers from a vending machine. He ate the crackers slowly, watching the girl working. She moved swiftly, piling up the clothes. She looked like she was still in school, maybe the same age as he was.

She began wiping the machines. If he had a job like this nobody would have to know he wasn't living at home. He could be working and living around here. If he could get a job for nights in a launderette, maybe he could sleep on a cot in the back.

"Closing time ten minutes," the girl said. "We close early on Saturday."

He finished his crackers and left. It was still raining. He looked up and down the street. On the corner the streetlights threw a fuzzy pool of light onto the sidewalk. No one was in sight. He walked down the street, putting up his thumb for every passing car. Water splashed up at him from the pavement. The wind cut through his wet jeans.

On the corner was a used-car lot. Big Bob's Bargain. He walked between the rows of cars, looking for one that was unlocked so he could wait out the rain inside; but everything was locked up tight. Shivering, his wet hair falling into his face, he kept going.

On the next block was another lot with trucks. He didn't expect anything, but he found an open van. He vaulted up onto the tailgate. It was dim in the truck, which was half filled with boxes smelling of soap. He shook himself like a dog and moved toward the back, out of the half-light. He was cold and wet to his skin. His teeth ached.

Outside he heard men talking. He hunkered down, out of sight. "Okay, Ron, you're all set." Footsteps approached. Now they would find him and kick him out. The rain drove noisily against the aluminum skin of the truck. His legs were trembling. Then the door to the back of the van was slammed shut. Someone entered the cab, and the engine turned over. Then the truck was moving. Boxes creaked. He braced himself against the side of the van. He was glad he was on his way somewhere. It didn't matter where. Going was all that mattered. Home, his mother, the warmth of their apartment, everything he'd ever loved was gone now, lost, out of reach.

He buried his face against his crossed arms. He hadn't planned for any of this, but that was okay. Plans were shit. All his plans had come to nothing. It was better this way, just moving along, just letting whatever was going to happen, happen.

Briefly he remembered the incredible sense of power and pride he'd felt when Richard had made his third broad jump. How he'd congratulated himself! *He* had made it happen, *he* had taught Richard, *he* was responsible for Richard's moment of glory.

And his own moment of glory, when he'd broken past Kinsella, when he was winning. *He* had made that happen, too. He closed his eyes. The glory was nothing now, shriveled and pale like a punctured balloon. He felt small, powerless, tired, and cold.

The tires whined steadily. He dozed off. When the truck stopped, the silence was sudden and stunning. The cab door opened, then banged shut. There was the scrape of footsteps on gravel, then the back doors were flung open. Hidden behind a stack of boxes, Willis waited tensely. The footsteps moved off.

He crept to the door. He saw a dimly lit platform, and a man in a yellow slicker wheeling a dolly toward him. He stepped out and dropped below the platform.

"You, there!" The man had seen him.

Darting beyond the light of the loading platform, Willis ran, and kept running till he was sure no one was after him. He was on a dark paved road. The wind blew through his wet clothes. In the distance he heard dogs barking.

He walked, then ran again, trying to warm himself. A cold gray mist covered the fields. Not a house in sight. He had never felt so completely miserable in his life.

The hum of a car approaching brought him to the side of the road, his thumb lifted. The car sped past. Ten or fifteen minutes later, another car passed him without even slowing. After that he stopped trying. Anyway, people would be sure to ask questions. What are you doing out here? Where do you live? Where are you going? He had no answers.

Heat flickered in his belly as he remembered his father staggering toward him on the track. He made his mind blank and trudged on, past rough fields and scrubby woods.

A long time later a building loomed up in the darkness. Two stories high, rows of boarded-up windows. An abandoned factory. In back Willis found a door rattling loose. He pushed it open. The door creaked, and a cold damp smell spilled out. Willis hestitated; then, shivering, he stepped into the darkness.

CHAPTER 16

Willis stood just inside the factory door. Beyond the short corridor in which he stood was a big vaulted room filled with the dim shapes of old machines. The wind sent a sheet of rain driving through the door, and Willis pushed it shut. He'd never been in such a dark place in his life. He slid down onto the floor, talking to himself. "Stay here till the rain stops. . . . " He listened. It was coming down as hard as ever.

He was cold; his wet clothes clung to his skin. The rain gusted against the building. He drew himself together, knees bent, arms around his chest. He kept very still, feeling the heat of his body slowly gathering beneath his clothes. From the big room next to him came the sound of creaking. It was hard not to be spooked.

For a long time he sat without moving, listening to the rain and the wind, listening and thinking. He tried to think carefully about the next day, about going on to wherever it was that he was going, but his eyes were heavy. He'd hitchhike, or maybe find another open truck. He'd need money . . . and food . . . a knapsack? His head sank down on his chest.

He dozed off. Faces paraded through his mind. His father, Richard, Mr. Hayfoot, Miss Herman . . . Then he was on a bus with his father. Mr. Hayfoot was driving. They were going downtown, then suddenly he looked down and his father was lying on the floor of the bus. It was slippery because everyone had come in with their wet shoes. Willis cried out. He thought his father was DOA. Then a woman explained to him that DOA meant Don't Order Anybody, and Willis said, "Then that's all right."

He woke up laughing with relief. For a moment he couldn't figure out where he was, why he was so uncomfortable. He shifted, tried lying down on the floor. Some crazy dream he'd had. He'd barely seen his father in the dream, but he knew it was him lying dead on the floor. And the sense of relief at the end had been terrific, he still felt it. The funny part was Mr. Hayfoot being a bus driver. He found himself wishing Richard were with him. Richard had a good sense of humor, and he liked stories. Willis could tell him the whole dream. He could just about hear Richard giggling. "Poppy driving a bus? That's funny, Willis."

Willis moved again, put an arm under his cheek, trying to find a comfortable way to lie on the floor. It was easy being around Richard, he thought, a little surprised by the idea. Richard didn't make a lot of demands, he didn't criticize you or think what you were doing or saying wasn't good enough. Just the opposite, really. He looked up to Willis, which was sometimes annoying, but sometimes pretty nice.

The wind rattled against the boarded-up windows. "Lie still," Willis told himself. His voice sounded puny in the darkness. If he didn't move, maybe he could forget how miserable he felt. He shivered. He wished he was sitting in front of a fire. Or on a beach somewhere. Maybe in Florida. He'd seen those Florida beaches on TV. The sun shone there about all the time. He could live on one of those beaches, maybe nail up a little shack in an old orange grove. He wouldn't bother anyone. Every day he'd go out on the beach and pick up things that had been washed up. Wood for his shack, maybe things to sell.

He'd fish, and then cook his catch over an open fire. And he'd pick oranges and grapefruit right off the trees. If he needed money he'd do errands for people. Maybe after a while he'd let Richard visit him. It could be good for Richard, living outdoors that way. He could teach Richard a lot of things. How to fish, how to build shelves, how to take care of himself. Taking care of yourself was the most important thing you ever had to learn.

Richard, he'd say, *you want people to respect you. You don't want anyone to push you around. So you have to live your life your own way. Take care of yourself. Make up your mind what you want to do, and then do it. Then nobody can boss you around.*

A sudden spasm of shivering caught him. His teeth clicked together uncontrollably. He finally stopped it by clamping his jaws shut and thinking about home. His own room, his bed, burrowing under twenty blankets, smothering under in all that heaviness and heat . . .

He was lying with his face on a floor. There was a gray morning light all around him. He lay there, thinking where he was. He sat up, wiped his mouth, and got stiffly to his feet. He must have slept finally, but his eyes felt as if someone had thrown handfuls of sand into them. He smoothed back his hair, shivering. His clothes were filthy and damp. He went outside hurriedly, glad to leave the building.

The sky had cleared. Far above a jet passed. Willis looked around at the flat unfamiliar landscape. The road passed through cleared fields. He was hungry, and he was thirsty, and he wished he could wash his eyes with cold water and brush his teeth. But he had to make plans. He couldn't just stand here feeling crummy. Well, he could go on walking, just keep walking till he got somewhere. He saw himself trudging this way forever through cold fields, driven out of his home by his father. His blood stirred. Damn him. Anger boiled in his belly. It was his home, too!

Suddenly he started down the road, going back the way he'd come. He wanted to go home. He *was* going home. As he walked, Field Day flashed through his mind, like a series of frozen stills. The gun going off . . . running . . . the track . . . the finish line like a door he couldn't miss . . . then his father. Strange how remote it had all begun to seem. Hard to believe it was only yesterday.

Behind him the sun hung just above the horizon. In the rain-cleared air he could hear a car coming a long way off. He walked backward, his thumb up, not expecting anything. The old pickup truck slowed down and stopped ahead of him. It was loaded with crates of eggs. Willis ran forward. "Where you going?" the driver said.

Willis hesitated. He could say anything, he could go anywhere. He could still change his mind. Then he heard himself saying, "I'm going home," and he felt it in the pit of his stomach. "The city," he added, his hand still on the door. "Is this the right way?"

"Sure is. Get in."

The driver was an older man wearing a plaid shirt. The truck smelled of coffee and cigarettes, a homey smell Willis enjoyed. "Where exactly in the city?" the driver said, easing the truck off the shoulder.

"Villa Street. That's the south side, off East Broadway."

"Oh, sure, I know that area. I deliver eggs all over the city. Nice fresh country eggs." He switched on the heater. Warm air blew up against Willis's legs.

Willis leaned back against the seat. Nothing had ever felt so good as that heat.

"Said you were going home?" the driver said. Willis nodded.

"Where you been, visiting?"

"Sort of." He rolled down the car window.

The driver was talking about how few people knew what real fresh eggs tasted like. "Big difference between my eggs and the ones you buy in the supermarket." Willis closed the window and sat back, half listening.

The driver let him off at the far end of East Broadway. All the little shops and stores were shuttered and closed. He walked through the silent Sunday-morning streets to his block. In their house, he went up the steps slowly, stopping at each landing to listen. But the entire building was quiet.

He unlocked the door to their apartment and entered quietly. "Willis?" His mother was in the living room in her pink bathrobe. He knew at once that she'd been waiting for him all night. She came to him and put her hands on his shoulders. Her eyes filled, then she kissed him on the cheek. "Are you all right?"

"Sure." He wrapped his arms around her waist like a little kid again and briefly leaned against her. Then he caught himself listening, and he knew what it meant. He was listening for his father. He pulled away. "Where's Pop?"

She pointed to the bedroom. Willis walked past her down the hall. He tapped on the wall, lightly at first, then louder, and louder still, announcing himself. *Here I am. Wake up. Here I am, back home.*

His father was lying on his bed covered with a blanket. "Pop," Willis said. His heart was pounding. His father opened his eyes, then sat up.

"You're home, ay?" They exchanged a glance. His father nodded, then lay back and closed his eyes. That was all there was to it.

Almost sick with relief, Willis went into the bathroom and stripped off his clothes. He stood under a hot shower, soaping himself and soaking up the heat. The room turned white with steam. He put on dry clean clothes and went into the kitchen. His mother had sausages cooking. She broke three eggs into the pan and put bread on the table. He wolfed down the food.

His mother sat down across from him. "Well, where were you?" she said.

He told her briefly. "Were you worried, Mom?"

"What do you think?" She lit a cigarette.

"And your father, too. We didn't sleep most of the night."

"I'm sorry," Willis said. His eyes were so heavy he could hardly hold them open. He was feeling strange. Time seemed to have stretched, so that Field Day had taken place far off in another time zone. And meanwhile, things here had been shrinking. Everything in the apartment, the rooms, the furniture, looked smaller. His father had looked so small lying under the covers.

He ate the last bit of egg. He pushed aside the dish and put his head down on the table. He heard his mother say, "Willis, what are you doing?" and then he fell asleep.

CHAPTER 17

Combing his hair in front of the mirror before school Monday morning, Willis thought of all the kids who had seen his father drunk on Saturday. Then he said to himself, *Well, so they know. So that's that.* He got his lunch money and books and left the apartment, locking the door behind him. His father had gone to work already, his mother was still asleep.

The morning passed uneventfully. No one said anything special to him. No one acted different. Kids were talking about Field Day, and he kept checking them out, waiting for the smart cracks about his boozy father. But there was nothing.

At noon when he entered the cafeteria he was still tense, still waiting for that crack. He got in line. Sue Tyson was ahead of him. To his surprise she turned and spoke to him. "Slow line today."

Willis nodded assent. The line shuffled forward. Sue turned again. "Good race Saturday," she said. "I thought you were going to win. You were in the lead."

Okay, here it comes, Willis thought. He made his face blank. Let her say whatever she wanted. He wasn't going to fall apart.

She shook her head. "You never can tell, can you? I mean, sometimes you do great, and sometimes, pffft!" She blew out her lips. "It happens to the best athletes."

Willis nodded mechanically, playing back what she'd said, looking for the hidden meaning. But there were no hidden meanings. And he realized she wasn't going to say anything. She must have seen his father. Everybody had seen him. But that's the way it had been all day, not a word. It was unbelievable.

Sue was bouncing up and down on her toes. She was wearing a skirt for a change, and he couldn't help looking at her legs. They were nice, sturdy and smooth. He wouldn't mind touching them. He caught himself thinking that and almost laughed out loud. Oh, no, getting horny over Sue Tyson.

She tapped him on the shoulder. "You going out for track next fall?" Willis shrugged. "You're good," Sue said. "You ought to." When he didn't say anything to this, she put her hands on her hips and said, "Listen, don't you *ever* talk?"

He reddened and said something dumb about being hungry. It dawned on him that she was really being friendly. She wasn't bringing up the cigar butt or any of the other dumb things he'd done.

A commotion in the far corner of the cafeteria caught his attention. Rabbit had arrived and was being greeted. Willis's lip curled. He would never get over hating Rabbit.

"Oh, that big conceited ape," Sue said, following his glance. "Do you like him?"

"Like poison," Willis said.

"Me, too," Sue said. "I don't see how a decent guy like Sam Viglione can hang around with that big ape."

"Oh, Viglione's kind of a junior ape," Willis said without thinking.

"I can see your point." She laughed as if he'd said something really funny. Having made her laugh once, he wanted to see her laugh again, but he couldn't think of anything else to say.

Then Richard came running up, his blue third-place ribbon pinned to the pocket of his shirt. "Willis, did you see my ribbon? Hi, Sue Tyson, this is the ribbon I won in Field Day for champion broad jumping."

"Yes, I saw your blue ribbon on Saturday, Richard. *And* the line starts at the rear." She pointed. "Thataway, bub."

"I have to talk to my friend." He squeezed in next to Willis.

Sue rolled her eyes. "I love you guys who butt in anyplace. Don't they teach you manners in your class?"

"I have good manners," Richard said. "I say please and thank you. Please, Willis, are we going to work out after school?"

Willis hadn't thought beyond Field Day. He'd been thinking his job was over. "What'd your father say?"

"Poppy says, 'You work out with Willis,'" Richard said, lowering his voice. "'You work out with Willis every day. Hear me, Richard?'"

"What do you do with him, Willis?" Sue said.

He liked hearing her say his name. He felt

excited and gave Richard a friendly jab in the arm. "Oh, calisthenics, running, stuff like that. I got him in shape for Field Day."

"Your own trainer, huh, Richard?" she said. "You lucky stiff." Richard smiled, pleased.

"I'll meet you in the usual place," Willis said, and Richard, satisfied, dropped to the back of the line.

Willis picked up a sandwich and a carton of milk. Sue took her tray to a table where a group of girls was sitting. Willis sat down at another table and opened his milk. He glanced over to where Sue was sitting with the other girls. Except for Marion, she was actually the cutest one in the whole bunch. He stared at Marion for a minute, then took a bite out of his sandwich. Richard joined him and began talking, but Willis hardly heard a word.

He was thinking that tomorrow he'd meet Sue after school. They'd go someplace and talk, and who knew what would happen after that? Once you started talking to a girl, it was just the beginning. A lot of things could happen. He finished his sandwich. Him and Sue Tyson. Why not!

CHAPTER 18

"Hungry?" his father said to Willis. It was Wednesday night, and this was the first word he'd said directly to Willis since Sunday morning. He was at the stove in his undershirt, sizzling a steak on the frying pan.

"I can eat," Willis said briefly. Not talking had been all right with him. All week he'd avoided his father. When they were in the house together he didn't look up to gauge the state of his father's spirits. Was he up or down? His father's silences, his moodiness—all his life, like knuckles in Willis's back. He didn't want that anymore. Call it selfishness. He could see the old story on his mother's face, that anxious pinched look around her eyes. He felt bad for her. She was still on the seesaw with his father. But he was off.

His father sliced potatoes and onions to fry, then cukes and tomatoes for the table. "Put out bread," he told Willis. "Margarine. Cups."

They ate in silence as they had a hundred times before. Willis cut his steak into little chunks, mixed the fried onions and potatoes together, then chewed, staring out the window.

"Willis—" His father lifted his hands, those dry mutilated fingers. "Our fight last week. I hit you again. I'm sorry. I said I'd never hit you again, and then I did it."

Willis's throat was dry. He looked across the table at his father. "I hit you back."

"I remember." His father shaded his eyes. "I remember something else, ay? You said something to me. I don't want to repeat it, I make believe you don't say it." There was a hopeful, uncertain half smile on his father's face. "I just hope you don't hate your father that much anymore."

Willis looked away. All his life he'd wanted to be proud of his father. He'd wanted to be

THE WAR ON VILLA STREET

close to his father. Sometimes it had happened. Now he was fighting it. *Leave me alone. Let me live my own life.* He looked out beyond the silhouette of the nearby rooftops. The sky was pale violet, bristling with a forest of TV antennas. Somewhere among those spare shapes, someone moved. Someone was up there on a roof. Willis imagined whoever it was could see Willis and Raymond through the window. They could see a father and his son sitting down to eat together. Two people who belonged together. He felt a dryness spread inside like sand swept bare and hard.

"I don't hate you, Pop."

His father put his hand over Willis's hand. "Then everything's all right. You're still my son. I knew it."

Willis felt the wind rushing to his throat, his eyes blurring, all his manly defenses, the sober assessment of his own strength, his new-found independence, collapsing. His father was getting to him again. He concentrated on the skyline.

Every moment of his life his father had been there in his mind, leaning on him, getting to him. It was either love or hate. He had never been free of his father. Where was his father? What was he doing? What were people saying about him? Was he drunk or sober, dead or alive?

No more. No more. Please, no more. He wanted to be free of all that. He had to be free, or he couldn't live. Oddly, thinking that, he felt sorry for his father. He pushed the donuts across the table. "Have one, Pop." He stood up. "I'm going out for a while."

"Where you going?"

"I don't know. Look around." Maybe he'd find a game on the street. Maybe he'd just walk around. He checked himself in the hall mirror and smoothed his hair. Maybe he'd run into Sue. He didn't know what was going to happen. He raced down the stairs. He was whistling when he reached the street.